M000195985

PRAISE FOR AN ANGEL FOR DADDY

"An Angel for Daddy is a toothachingly sweet story! Lovers of romance centering hot single dads will have their appetites whet with this gem of a tale!"

- Nicole Falls, Author of *F*ck and Fall in Love*

"I devoured this beautiful, hot and touching novella. Ruby and Spencer had undeniable chemistry and Nina was just adorable. I loved it."

- Janine Caroline, Author of *I Look at You and Smile*

"Their first kiss will make you sigh & vow to finish the book in one sitting. FIVE BIG STARS OF HELL YES."

- Rebel Carter, Author of *Heart and Hand*

"DEAR ROMANCELANDIA, PLEASE READ AN ANGEL FOR DADDY BY LUCY EDEN. PLEASE, I IMPLORE YOU"

PRAISE FOR LUCY EDEN

EVERYTHING'S BETTER WITH YOU

"Everything's Better With You is a rare gem in the romance novel world. It has depth, great characters and a totally believable story line."

- The Laundry Librarian

EVERYTHING'S BETTER WITH KIMBERLY

"Engaging with attention to detail and kept me hooked from start to finish."

- Janine Caroline, Author of I Look at You and Smile

CHERISHING THE GODDESS

"The perfect balance of humor, angst, and steam. Highly recommended!"

- PE Kavanaugh, Author of Sex, Money and the Price of Truth

"This enemies to lovers romance will make your insides roar and you will want to pick up Lucy Eden's backlist immediately."

- Silvana Reyes, Frolic Media

ALSO BY LUCY EDEN

Cover Design: Lucy Eden

Cover Illustration: Hellhoney

Nina's Family Drawing: Genevieve D.

Every story is for my mom, who made me fall in love with reading & Ms. K, who made me fall in love with writing.

AN ANGEL FOR DADDY

Spencer & Ruby have plenty of reasons to stay apart, but can a little divine intervention & an assist from a pint-sized cupid teach them a lesson that will last a lifetime?

Ruby Hayes is intelligent, beautiful, great at her job, and loves her students.

She's not too fond of me because despite moving to this small coastal California town only a month ago, I've managed to get on her bad side by consistently arriving late to pick up my daughter, Nina. It's probably for the best. Between my job & adjusting to raising a little girl by myself, adding romance to the equation isn't something I have time for.

Spencer Jones is successful, handsome, a doting father, and terrible at reading a clock.

His daughter, Nina also happens to be my favorite student. Getting involved with the parent of a student is a bad idea, no matter how witty & charming they might be. It's probably for the best. Between my job, taking care of my dad & climbing out of debt, a new relationship is the last thing I need.

AN ANGEL FOR DADDY

LUCY EDEN

ONE

RUBY

"You're old," Nina, my newest student, informed me as she dug her fingers into another pot of paint.

"I'm not old. I'm twenty-seven," I replied as I continued to tidy up my classroom while Nina worked.

Nina's eyes went wide as saucers, and she paused mid-finger-painting stroke.

"I'm five, and I'm a big girl," she explained. "So, twenty-seven is old." She nodded and turned back to her painting of what she told me was an elephant but more closely resembled a green blob. I guessed the matter was settled.

I went back to tidying up the art supplies while we waited for Nina's dad to pick her up. This wasn't the first time he'd been late, and it probably wasn't the last. It was frustrating and annoying, but the look on Nina's face as she watched her classmates leave one by one was the worst.

So, nearly every day after school, I would volunteer to stay with her, distract her really, until her dad showed up. Today we were finger-painting.

"Hey, Little Bit!" a deep voice called from the doorway of my classroom.

"Daddy!" Nina squealed and took off running in the direction of the impossibly tall, disturbingly handsome, and mahogany-hued man leaning on my doorjamb. She leaped into his arms and wrapped her arms around his neck, leaving a gray and purple handprint on his suit. He laughed. "Oops, sorry, Daddy!"

"That's okay, baby girl. That is what dry cleaners are for." He set her down on her feet. "Get your stuff."

Nina took off, running to her cubby.

"Hey, Ms. Hayes. Thank you again for staying with Nina. I had a meeting that ran—"

"You know that pick-up time is three thirty."

"Yes, but as I said—"

"You know that because I told you on Tuesday when you showed up at four forty-two." I crossed my arms and glared at him.

"Wow, it's like that." He smirked at me, threatening to give me a glimpse of his perfect teeth. "Not a quarter to five or four forty-five. You hit me with the exact minute."

"Well, I thought it was imperative that you fully understood how much of an inconvenience it is when you're late picking up Nina."

"Again, I'm sorry. Please also apologize to your husband for me." His eyes flitted to my left hand, and I shoved it in the pocket of my skirt.

"Really?" I rolled my eyes. He smiled sheepishly, and Nina came running back to us, carrying her jacket and backpack.

"Hey, Daddy. Miss Ruby is old too."

"Is she?" He raised his eyebrows and shot me a glance, still smiling.

"She's not as old as you and Grandma, but she is way older than me."

"I'm not as old as Grandma, sweetie." He chuckled.

"Grandma is fifty-seven, Grandpa is sixty, Auntie Simi is thirty-five, you are thirty." He shot me an exasperated glance in reaction to Nina's words. "Mommy was twenty-five when she went to heaven, and I'm five."

His face fell, and the mood in the room shifted. Nina had only been in my class for a month. I assumed she was being raised by a single dad because I'd never seen anyone else pick her up, but I didn't know she'd lost her mom. I'd been so overwhelmed lately that I was now kicking myself for not going over Nina's file more closely. She also had an affinity for angels, and I was disappointed in myself for not making the connection. It was also a little surprising that she never mentioned it during our after-school hangout sessions. I was replaying every interaction, wondering if there were clues I missed or hoping to God I didn't say anything hurtful or insensitive.

"Okay, sweetie," her dad said in a sigh. "Great job remembering all those ages. Let's go home."

"But my painting…" She pointed at the easel.

"It's still drying, Nina. You can get it tomorrow. I'll keep it safe, and I'll make sure you remember to take it home." I smiled at her.

"Thanks again, Miss Hayes. I'll see you tomorrow at three thirty."

"Yup," I sighed and nodded, trying to sound cheerful but feeling like a complete asshole. "Three thirty."

He nodded and turned with Nina's tiny hand wrapped in his big one before leaving my classroom.

"Daddy," Nina said in a terrible imitation of a whisper. "Miss Ruby is twenty-seven."

"Oh, yeah?" He tossed a glance over his shoulder. It was at that moment that I realized that I'd been staring at them walk away. It was also the same moment that I'd realized he was going to catch me watching them walk away, and there was no way to prevent it. We locked eyes for a moment. I gave a small awkward wave and smiled with a little nod.

"Yes." Nina nodded seriously. "She's old like you."

"Hey, Daddy! I'm here. Sorry I'm late." I rushed into the living room and threw my tote bag and coat in the armchair on my way to the kitchen.

"Would you calm down, Ruby? The house isn't on fire." Dad was sitting on the couch, watching an episode of *Columbo*.

"Not this time," I muttered under my breath.

"That happened once," he said.

"Once is too many." I wrapped my arms around his shoulders and kissed him on my way to the kitchen. I opened the fridge and started pulling out ingredients. "What do you want for dinner: roasted chicken or spaghetti with meatballs?"

"Are you planning on seasoning the chicken?" His face was screwed up when I turned to look at him.

"Are you insulting my cooking? You know you can't have salt anymore."

"Hmm," was the response I got, so I resumed dinner prep. I reached behind the stove and turned the gas valve to the "on" position. I plugged in the oven and fished the stovetop knobs out of the cabinet under the sink where I'd hidden them. Within fifteen minutes, I had water boiling for rice and chopped vegetables with two lightly seasoned chicken breasts arranged in a roasting pan sitting on the middle rack of the oven.

"So, did you give any thought to that senior living community?" I was setting the table and doing my best to feign nonchalance. My dad was the strongest person I'd ever known, but he was just as stubborn. The longer he chose to ignore his deteriorating condition, the more I worried about him being alone.

"No, I did not. I do not need to live in no old folks' rest home." He huffed out a mirthless chuckle.

"Dad, it's not an old folks' home." I seated myself beside him and clasped his hand. "I just worry about you here all day by yourself."

"I'm not by myself." He brought my hand to his lips. "I have you." He smiled at me. "I've been taking care of us all this time. That isn't going to change anytime soon."

I squeezed his hand and stood to finish making dinner, but also so he couldn't see how his words affected me. Losing my mother was hard on us both, but there was never a moment in my life when I needed my father and he wasn't there for me. My eyes began to sting with tears.

I knew that things would be changing sooner than later. My dad's recovery after his stroke was nothing short of miraculous, but that stroke was brought on by years of working too much, eating poorly, smoking, and the stress of being a single father raising a girl.

After weeks in the hospital, following many months of rehab. Dad had become forgetful. He was also resentful of his strict lifestyle changes and loss of independence.

I had no problem moving in with him. My old room was still untouched, and I was able to give up my apartment, freeing up a sizable chunk of my salary. Though I had no hope of ever paying off my student loan debt, it was nice not to have to endure the daily calls. I would be roommates with my dad forever if I could, but his condition was quickly becoming unmanageable, and I hated even leaving him to go to work.

"Dad, you should let me hire a home health aide to stay with you during the day?"

"Ruby, I don't need a babysitter. And it's too expensive."

"Your insurance will cover most of it. I'll cover the rest."

"No. You won't. Your money is for you. Stop fussing over me and feed me some of that bland-ass chicken and that nasty sugar-free ice tea." He laughed, and I joined him.

"Fine," I conceded and set a plate in front of him before joining him at the table. "This isn't over."

"So, why were you getting home so late again? Same fella late picking up his daughter?"

"Yes." I nodded and cast my eyes down at my plate, not wanting to look Dad in the eye. I was suddenly ashamed of all of the times I'd complained about him to my father, remembering how much my dad struggled to raise me and work a full-time job. I depended a lot on my aunts and cousins, especially when it came to things my dad couldn't help me with. I had no idea what Nina's father must be dealing with, and I felt bad for judging him.

"I'll bet he keeps coming around after everyone's gone because he's sweet on you."

I laughed.

"Dad, maybe that worked in your day, but they call that stalking now, and it's no longer cute. It's illegal."

"I'm just sayin'…" He laughed and took a bite of his chicken, chewing a couple times before leaning his head to the side. "Not bad, Peanut. What's different?"

"A pinch of Lawry's."

"That's my girl. Lawry's makes everything better." He laughed.

"But just a pinch."

"How about a pinch of hot sauce?" He raised his eyebrows at me with a cunning smirk.

"No way."

"Fine."

TWO

SPENCER

"Daddy?" Nina was wearing a beard made of bath suds.

"What's up, Little Bit?" I was sitting on the edge of the bathtub with my sleeves rolled up to the elbows.

"Do you think Miss Ruby is pretty?" she asked.

Nina's big brown eyes bored into me the way her mother's used to. She asked me a question while simultaneously reading my face to get her own answer.

"Why are you asking?"

Good job, Spencer. Answer all questions you don't want to answer with a question until she gets distracted.

"Because you were looking at her today like you thought she was pretty."

Shit. This kid doesn't miss anything.

I took a deep breath and let out a sigh. I didn't think it was possible to look at Ruby Hayes without looking at her like she was pretty. She was breathtaking.

She was tall, slim, but with the kind of hips that you could curve the palm of your hand around while you danced. Her hair was a crown of reddish-brown coils. Her skin was the color of bronze, and cocoa butter kissed, making it glow. The rare occasion I'd heard her laugh, it was like a musical tinkling of bells. She didn't smile at me, but I could tell she really cared about Nina. I hadn't looked at anyone like that since we lost Sarai, and it felt good, but also strange. And to know that Nina noticed and was now asking questions was starting to make my head hurt.

I also wondered about the ring on her finger. When I asked about it, she didn't give me an answer, and she hid it.

What was that about?

"Daddy?" Most of Nina's bubble beard had fallen away, and she was still staring at me, waiting for a response.

"Yes, Nina. I think Miss Ruby is pretty. But I also think you are pretty, and I also think you are ready to rinse your hair and get out of the tub."

She groaned. I inwardly groaned. Combing Nina's hair wasn't fun for either of us. I dunked the back of her head in the tub to rinse out the conditioner and ran the wide-toothed comb through it to detangle it. Then I parted it into two sections and plaited them into two braids. We'd gotten the semi-weekly routine down to twenty-five minutes.

I let her play with her tub toys while the water drained before wrapping her in a terry cloth robe. I let her lotion herself and put on her pajamas.

"—WHERE MAX'S DINNER WAS STILL WAITING FOR him," I said, preparing to close her favorite bedtime story.

"And it was still hot," she finished.

"The End," we said in unison.

"Goodnight, Daddy." She blew me a kiss. "Goodnight, Mommy." She blew a kiss to Sarai's photo on her dresser.

"Goodnight, Little Bit."

I pulled the door closed, but not completely shut.

"I found her," I heard Nina whisper.

"What, baby?" I poked my head in the room.

"I wasn't talking to you, Daddy."

"Who were you talking to?"

"Mommy."

"Ah, okay," I said. Nina's therapist noted that it was healthy for kids who've lost parents to talk to their photos. Lord knows I spoke to Sarai a lot in the months after I lost her.

"Daddy, can I watch one of Mommy's videos?"

"Not tonight, but you can watch one in the car on the way to school tomorrow."

"Okay," she sighed, then she yawned. I tapped the doorframe with my knuckle and went downstairs. I envied the way Nina was handling losing her mother. The loss was a sharp pain I walked around with all day. The almost two years she'd been gone had dulled the edges, but the ache never went away.

I SAT AT THE KITCHEN ISLAND, POURED MYSELF TWO fingers of Jim Beam, and opened my laptop to work. Losing Sarai and having to raise Nina alone put a lot of things in perspective for me. I was working too much and spent too much time away from my family. When I still had a family.

Determined not to let that happen again, I took a job across the country that would pay my asking rate but allow me to spend half of my time working from home.

I was able to drop Nina off in the morning, and go to the office and pick her up after school. It meant working into the wee hours of the morning and not getting a ton of sleep, but it was worth it. It was also incredibly unhealthy, and I wasn't sure how long I could keep it up. It also didn't do anything to assuage the guilt of not doing it while Sarai was still alive, but I think she would be proud of the way I was taking care of Nina. I was trying, at least.

I FINISHED THREE REPORTS BEFORE MY EYES STARTED to glaze over. I looked at my watch. It was late in California, which meant it was later in Chicago. I took a chance that my sister would still be awake.

"Spence, what's up? Is Nina okay?" Simi's voice was groggy and thick with sleep.

"Yeah, Sim, she's fine."

"So why are you calling me at three in the morning?"

"I think I fucked up." I took a sip of my whiskey.

"Fucked up what?"

"I think I flirted with Nina's kindergarten teacher."

"I'm gonna kill you." She sighed.

"C'mon, sis. I need advice."

"You called me in the middle of the night to tell me you flirted with someone? Spence, Sarai has been gone for almost two years. Is it so out of the ordinary for you to be attracted to someone else? Especially a woman who takes care of your daughter."

"Nina noticed, and she's asking questions. I'm not ready to date, and you know how she is. She's tenacious like her mother. Lord knows what she's telling this woman about me."

"Do you care?" she asked.

"Of course, I care, but not the way you're thinking. I mean, I don't care. Okay, I care a little bit." I didn't know what the hell I was saying. I took another sip of my whiskey.

"Mm-hmm. You care so little that you're waking people up to tell them how little you care." Simi sounded like she was wearing one of Mom's sarcastic expressions, and I missed not being in the same city as her.

"I care about Nina, and I don't want her getting confused or upset or getting her hopes up. I don't know."

"Tell me about this teacher. Is she cute?"

"Yes, she's cute. She's beautiful, but I'm not her favorite person."

"What did you do already? You just moved there a month ago."

"I've been late picking up Nina a couple of times," I said. I listened to Simi's weighted pause before adding, "Okay, more than a couple of times. I'm getting used to working part-time. Her school doesn't have an after-school program." I wouldn't enroll her even if it did.

"Why don't you hire a babysitter or a nanny?"

"Hell no, Simi." My incredulous laugh sounded like a bark. "Ma would never let me hear the end of it. She was pissed that I moved Nina halfway across the country. How would she react if she found out that I hired a stranger in California to do what she would do for free in Illinois?"

"You need to stop thinking about what's best for Ma and worry about what's best for you and Nina. We didn't need nannies when we were kids. We could take care of ourselves. We had aunties and cousins and neighbors. It's not like it was when we were kids. Do you even know your neighbors?"

"Nope."

"Exactly. Just hire someone to pick Nina up from school and watch her for a couple of hours until you get home."

"That's good advice, but I'm gonna try to figure out a way to do it on my own. I'm not ruling it out, but the whole point of this move was to spend as much time with Nina as possible."

"Okay, little brother. Just make sure you're doing what's best for you and Nina and not punishing yourself for things you can't change."

"Okay. I hear you."

"But are you listening?"

"Yes." I laughed. "But I think you have that backward."

"I said what I said," she replied, "and keep flirting with cute women, but maybe not your daughter's teacher. It's time. Sarai would want you and Nina to be happy. You know that."

"Yeah, I know."

"I love you, Spencer, but if you call me again at three in the morning for nonsense, I'm flying to Cali and beating your ass."

I let out a belly laugh, and Simi joined me.

"I love you, too."

"I'm proud of you, little brother. Go to bed."

"Okay."

I swallowed the last of my whiskey, chased it with a glass of water, and took my sister's advice.

THREE

"That's a beautiful necklace, Nina." My after-school buddy held up a ring of pink yarn threaded through about twenty painted penne noodles. "Who's that for?"

"I made it for you." She held it out to me. "It's a thank-you gift. I know my daddy is always late, and you always wait with me, and I know you don't have to."

My heart broke at her declaration. The pieces melted as I took the necklace from her and slipped it over my head.

"Do you like it?" she asked.

"I love it. It's beautiful, just like you."

Her face lit up.

"Hey, Little Bit." Nina's dad stood in the doorway. He looked out of breath and a little disheveled. A glance at the clock told me it was almost four. He was earlier than usual, but still late.

"Daddy!" Nina did her usual squeal and ran into her dad's arms. He set her down, and she ran in the direction of her cubby.

"I know. I know." He held up his hands in concession. "I know I'm late again. I really tried this time."

"Are you implying you didn't try the other times?" I smirked at him.

"What? No, I mean, I scheduled my meetings so I would have plenty of time to get here—" he stammered.

"It's okay. Really. I don't mind staying with Nina. She's a great kid." I offered what I hoped was a kind smile.

"Oh." His face fell. "I see."

"What?"

"That face."

"What face?"

"You had no problem putting me in my place before you found out I was a widower and a single parent, but now you're giving me 'the face.'"

My face went slack, and I could feel the heat rising in my neck and cheeks. I quickly schooled my expression and continued, a little annoyed, "So now you're upset that I'm cutting you a little slack."

"No, I'm upset that you're pitying me."

"I'm not pitying you. I just—" I wasn't sure how I was going to end that sentence because I was pitying Spencer Jones. My feelings about him picking up Nina late every day had definitely changed in the days since I found out about his wife. I'd looked forward to spending time with Nina, remembering how much I treasured spending time with women when I was her age. Luckily for me, Nina came back from her cubby and saved me.

"Here, Daddy." She held up a nearly identical macaroni necklace, but this one was blue. "I made this for you."

He took it from her with a massive grin on his face that faltered slightly when he noticed the one I was wearing.

"This is awesome. Thank you."

"You have to wear it now," she commanded. He reluctantly put it over his head. "Okay, you have to stand next to Miss Ruby so I can take a picture and send it to Auntie Simi."

"Sweetie, I don't think that's a good idea." He shot me a quick glance.

"My aunt Simi makes necklaces as her job," she informed me. "I wanted to show her mine. Maybe if she likes them, she can sell them in her store." She turned to address her father. "You and Miss Ruby are my models."

She grinned at him, and I could see the moment he relented. Nina must get her way a lot by flashing that grin.

"I'm sorry," he said to me.

"Hey, I can't discourage a young entrepreneur, and I've always wanted to be a model... I'm too short," I joked, but he didn't smile. His reaction made my heart thud, and I tried to keep my face placid.

Nina's dad handed her his phone, and she directed us. We stood next to each other, and I was close enough to smell his spicy, woodsy cologne mixed with the faint hint of sweat. I had gone from rudeness, to pity, to now wanting to climb this man like a tree. He turned to me, and our eyes met. We held that gaze for a few moments when I heard the click of the phone shutter.

"Okay. One more," our little photographer called out. We posed again, and Nina snapped a few more photos.

"Thank you, Miss Hayes." His parting greeting was curt, abrupt. And that same guilty feeling crept in, but this time it had brought a friend, frustration.

I was supposed to feel guilty for telling him off for being late and feel guilty for not telling him off for being late. This wouldn't even be an issue if he just got his butt here on time.

I shook it off and decided to head home. If I got Dad his dinner early, maybe I could convince my best friend to come out for a drink.

"Okay, first things first," Sabrina said and wrapped her perfectly manicured hand around her martini glass to take another sip of her cosmo. "What is his name?"

"Why?" I asked and sipped my cabernet.

"We are going to do a search for him." She pulled out her phone. She had her thumbs poised, and eyebrows raised. Sabrina was waiting for me to answer.

"Spencer Jones," I said in a low voice and took another sip of wine, a bigger sip.

"Spencer Jones? That sounds sexy as fuck." Her thumbs flew over her screen. She flipped the phone around to show me a screen full of photos of what I guessed were men name Spencer Jones. I scrolled until I found Nina's dad and clicked. She turned the phone around. "Oh, Rube, he is fine...and smart... and rich...and a widower."

"I know he's a widower. Are you satisfied with your search? This feels invasive." I took another sip of my wine. "I just wanted your opinion on how I should've handled today. I thought I was doing a good thing by not giving him a hard time when he obviously tried to be on time, but apparently, that wasn't the right thing to do."

"Well…" She cast one last glance at her phone before placing it facedown on the bar. "Remember when your mom died?" she asked. I nodded. "And you told me that everyone was fussing over you, and constantly talking about her, asking you how you were feeling and blah, blah, blah…" She waved her hand around.

"Yes, everyone except for you. You treated me like a regular person." I put my hand on top of hers and squeezed.

"Exactly." She nodded. "His wife died two years ago," she said. I blinked at her in surprise, and she pointed to her phone. "He wants to be treated like a person and not someone wearing a t-shirt that says *My Wife is Dead and I'm a Single Dad*. Treat him the way you wanted people to treat you."

I nodded and smiled at her.

"When are you planning on taking off that ring and stop scaring men away?" She held up her cosmo and pointed her head at my ring.

I reached for my mother's wedding ring and twisted it in response to Sabrina's question. I started wearing it during my first year of teaching. It doesn't work completely when it comes to fending off unwanted advances, but I've definitely seen men and women switch gears when they notice it. I haven't dated anyone since college, and with work and Dad keeping me busy, I don't really have time to think about a relationship. I tried online dating, but the three dating app setups were disastrous, and no amount of therapy would scrub away the memories of some of the messages I'd read or the number of unsolicited dick pics I'd been sent.

"He asked me if I was married," I said in a low voice.

"What did you say?" she said in a singsong voice.

"I deflected and hid my hand." I rolled my eyes.

"Mature, Ruby," she muttered and glared at me. "You seriously need to dust that thing off and see if it still works." She gestured to my waist. I was mid-sip and almost snorted wine through my nose. "But not with one of your students' parents. You don't want to be *that* teacher."

I laughed.

"How's Pop?" she asked. I've known Sabrina since we were Nina's age. Our mothers were best friends. When I lost my mom, we became closer. She moved to LA right after high school and became a highly sought-after event producer, but she moved back to help her mom two years ago.

"He's still pretty good. He's deteriorating, and he's being really stubborn about the assisted living facilities I've been trying to get him into."

"That's a big change. Ask me how I know." She took another sip of her drink.

"I know, but I'm scared. Dad's already set one fire. Yes, it was an accident, but I'm terrified to leave him alone, and he won't let me hire a home health aide."

"I'm sorry, babe. Let me know if there's anything I can do to help."

"Well, same. How's Aunt Anita?" I said, hoping to shift my thoughts away from my stubborn father.

"She's doing a lot better. The rehab went well, and she's settling into the new community."

"Oh, please tell me everything. Maybe if Aunt Anita likes it, she can talk to Daddy."

"Girl." She pursed her red-glossed lips, dropped her chin and glared at me, before signaling the bartender for another drink. "They are not lying when they say caring for an aging parent is like raising a child."

"What do you mean?" I thought I had an idea what she meant, taking care of Dad, but I felt like Sabrina was about to shock me, which was kind of my best friend's specialty.

"Hold on." She polished off her martini just as the bartender dropped off a fresh one. "I had to give my mother…a sex talk."

"What?" I whispered.

"Yes, girl." She slapped my thigh. "And condoms."

"In an assisted living community?"

"Yes," she hissed. "Those old folks get it in. Do you hear me?"

"Oh my God. Let me know where so I can keep Dad away from that one."

"Ruby." She put her hand on mine. "It's all of them. Those old folks are getting more action than both of us."

She laughed, and I joined her. It felt good to relax and have a sounding board. I loved having Sabrina home, though I felt a little guilty, being that the reason she came back was that her mom broke her hip.

"You okay, Ruby?"

"Yeah." I nodded. The word okay was the perfect descriptor. I wasn't happy, but I wasn't sad. I was under a lot of stress, but I still had a lot to be thankful for. I felt like something was missing, but I didn't have time to figure out what it was. "How about you, Brina?"

"Girl, same. I took a leave of absence that was supposed to be six months, which turned into two years. Now, I'm freelancing to make ends meet. Don't even get me started on dating. Why do men think everyone wants to see pictures of their dick?"

I snorted, laughing again.

"Okay. That's it," I said and picked up my glass. "No more stressing about men, our jobs, and our parents. This is girls' night."

Sabrina held up her cosmo and clinked our glasses.

"Deal, but only for the next two hours."

FOUR

SPENCER

My phone pinged for the third time in a row during the meeting.

"Do you need to get that?" Jason, another analyst, asked.

"No, it's fine. It's my sister. If it were an emergency, she'd call." I quickly set the phone to vibrate and stuffed my cell into my pocket.

"Can you turn off your phone?" he asked.

"Not with a five-year-old in school." I smiled at him because I didn't want to seem hostile, but there was no way I was cutting off communication with Nina, even for ten minutes. Simi was going to get an earful after my meeting. Jason conceded, and we continued the rest of the meeting without incident.

I waited until I was in the office to check my text messages. My breath caught in my throat when I opened the app. Nina must have sent her aunt the photos she took of Miss Hayes and me last week.

Big Head: What is going on here?

Me: I don't know what you mean.

Simi sent another photo. She'd zoomed on the picture of the two of us, locking eyes and circled our heads in red.

Big Head: this. You are eye fucking your daughter's teacher. And she is not cute, she's gorgeous.

Simi was always great at pointing out the obvious. My mind flashed back to every up-close encounter I had with Ruby Hayes, remembering every bounce of her curls and curve of her slim yet shapely body.

Me: You're supposed to be looking at the merchandise, not the models.

BIG HEAD: THESE NECKLACES ARE TOO CUTE. THEY'VE GIVEN ME AN IDEA FOR A NEW COLLECTION, BUT SEND ME ONE OF NINA'S CREATIONS. I'LL PUT IT IN A DISPLAY CASE AND TAKE A PICTURE FOR HER.

ME: SHE WOULD BE SO EXCITED.

BIG HEAD: YOU KNOW I LOVE THAT GIRL. NOW ANSWER MY QUESTION, LITTLE BROTHER. ARE YOU HOT FOR TEACHER?

Yes.

ME: THAT WOULD BE INAPPROPRIATE.

BIG HEAD: STILL NOT AN ANSWER. BUT I'LL TELL YOU SOMETHING. IF SANDRA AND I EVER LOOKED AT EACH OTHER THE WAY YOU TWO ARE LOOKING AT EACH OTHER IN THIS PHOTO, WE'D STILL BE MARRIED. JUST SAYING.

While I was contemplating how to answer her, I glanced at the clock. It was two forty-five. If I left now, I'd have a good chance of getting to Nina's school on time.

ME: SIM, I GOTTA GO. I'M GONNA BE ON TIME PICKING UP LITTLE BIT FOR ONCE. I'LL PUT MY NECK-LACE IN THE MAIL TOMORROW. THANKS AGAIN, LOVE YOU.

Big Head: Love you too.

It was three twenty-five when I pulled into the school parking lot. Parents of older kids had to wait in the pick-up line, but parents of kindergarten and preschool students were required to physically enter the building.

I signed in and headed for the classroom. It was precisely three thirty when I leaned on the door and caught Miss Hayes' eyes. She displayed a quick expression of shock, which quickly dissipated, and she called for Little Bit.

"Nina, your dad's here."

"Daddy," she squealed and crashed into me. "Why are you early?"

"I'm not early, baby, I'm on time." I shot a glance at Miss Hayes, who still wore her look of indifference. I turned to face her. "I'm on time for a change. I thought you'd be happy."

"You're supposed to be on time, Mr. Jones. Do you want me to applaud you for doing what you should be doing anyway?" She turned to me and raised an eyebrow. I was taken aback by her response, but I couldn't hold back a grin.

"Ah, so we've moved past pity. Good." I chuckled.

Her expression softened, and she turned to face me.

"Look. I owe you an apology— Goodbye, Hector. See you tomorrow." She waved to a little boy and his parents as they exited the classroom. "Everyone handles grief differently, and it's hard to gauge what someone does or doesn't need. What I'm trying to say is that it's hard to know how to react." Her hands were moving, and I looked down to see that she was fidgeting with her fingers, a nervous gesture. I also noticed she no longer wore a wedding ring.

"I lost my mother when I was a little older than Nina, and my dad raised me alone. It wasn't always easy for him, so I was really trying to give you the benefit of the doubt, but I was also pitying you, and I'm sorry." She sighed and offered me a hopeful smile that made me want to wrap my arms around her and kiss it off of her face. I pushed the thought away and took a deep breath.

"Well," I cleared my throat. "Thank you for saying that. Honestly, it has been really hard, with moving across the country. We don't have any friends or family on the West Coast. We're still trying to get the hang of our new normal. I shouldn't have been so harsh with you. You were trying to be nice, and you've been so helpful with Nina. You're all she ever talks about."

"I like her too." She smiled at Nina, and I felt myself smiling at her. I looked down to see Nina smiling at both of us. Her little face was lit up like a Christmas tree, and her eyes were darting between us like she was watching a tennis match.

"You ready, Little Bit?" I asked.

"Daddy, can Miss Hayes come over for dinner?" she asked.

I formed my lips to tell her that no, Miss Hayes couldn't come over for dinner, but I couldn't do it. I'd be lying if I said I didn't mind the idea of spending more time with her and if it was Nina's idea…I looked over at her trying to gauge her reaction to the question.

We stared at each other, and the seconds passed, making it more and more awkward until finally, she spoke.

"Thank you very much for the invitation, but I have to go home and have dinner with my dad." She smiled.

"You live with your daddy, too?" Nina's eyes sparkled.

"Yes, and he'd be really sad if he had to eat dinner alone, but thank you so much for inviting me." She flicked a quick glance at me before returning her attention to my tenacious offspring.

"He can come to dinner too," Nina suggested. Miss Hayes looked to me for help.

"Come on." I patted her head. "Let's let Miss Hayes get home. Maybe she'll come over for dinner another time."

"Sure, another time," Miss Hayes said.

"When?" Nina asked. She'd planted her feet and crossed her arms, looking up at us defiantly. I bent down, scooped her around the waist and flung her over my shoulder, and walked out of the classroom.

"See you tomorrow, Nina," Miss Hayes called behind us.

I BUCKLED HER INTO HER CAR SEAT, GOT IN THE driver's seat, and started the engine.

"What was that?" I caught her eye in the rearview mirror.

"What?" Nina shrugged and tried to hit me with her best version of an innocent grin.

"Why were you trying so hard to get Miss Hayes to have dinner with us?"

"I like her, Daddy," she answered matter-of-factly. "Don't you like her?"

How the hell was I supposed to answer that question? I did like her. I liked her in ways that would be inappropriate for a five-year-old to understand.

"I think she's very nice, and I like that you like her."

"But you said you think she's pretty." Her face furrowed. Pretty was an understatement.

"I do, but it's complicated, sweetie."

"What does complicated mean?" she asked.

I inwardly groaned. "It means it's hard for me to explain."

"So how I'm supposed to know if you can't explain it?"

I didn't answer her right away.

How could I explain it when I didn't understand it myself?

We drove the rest of the way home in silence, and when I pulled into the driveway, I sat in the car, gripping the steering wheel, lost in thought.

I was mad at myself for having feelings like this about someone I barely knew. It hadn't even been two years since Sarai had gone. What's even more frustrating is that Nina is now playing matchmaker. She'd lost her mother. I'd taken her away from all of the people she knows and loves. Of course, she's latched on to her teacher. Everything about this situation is f—

"Daddy, are you okay?" Nina's voice interrupted my train of thought.

"Yes, sweetie." I blinked and refocused. "Let's go inside."

Nina planted herself in front of the television in the living room and was watching cartoons while I seated myself at the kitchen island where I could keep an eye on her. I pulled out my phone and opened the text app to look at the photo of Ruby Hayes and me. I still remembered how it felt to be pinned by her deep chestnut-colored gaze. Something electric passed between us in those few seconds that felt like a lifetime. I never thought I'd feel that way about anyone again, and when I did, it was with the one person in this new town that I should stay away from. I dismissed the photo and decided to get started on dinner. I thought back to Nina and Miss Hayes' conversation.

"Thank you very much for the invitation, but I have to go home and have dinner with my dad."

"You live with your daddy, too?"

"Yes, and he'd be really sad if he had to eat dinner alone, but thank you so much for inviting me."

She lived with her dad, and she made him dinner every night. It made me curious about her, well, more curious than usual.

I realized that I was daydreaming about Nina's teacher while I stared into the refrigerator with the door open for ten minutes. I slammed the door and called out to Nina.

"Hey, do you want to go out for dinner instead of eating at home?"

"Yes!" she squealed. "Yes, yes, yes! But when this episode of Super Hero Girls is over."

THERE WAS A RESTAURANT ON THE WAY TO OUR HOUSE named Manny's that I knew would have things that Nina would eat.

"Table for two, please," I told the hostess.

"Miss Ruby," Nina called, and I looked up to see that Nina's teacher was waiting for a table with an older brown-skinned gentleman that had to be her father.

"Hi, Nina. What are you doing here?"

"We're having dinner. Is this your daddy? Do you want to sit with us?"

"Well, hello, little lady," Ruby's father bent low and addressed Nina. "Who might you be?"

"I'm Nina. Miss Ruby is my teacher, and this is my dad." She slipped her little hand into my big one and tugged it, along with the rest of my body towards Miss Hayes and her father. I extended my hand.

"Spencer Jones, sir."

"Jack Hayes." His grip was firm, and his eyes narrowed at me as if he were sizing me up. Still gripping my hand, he turned his head towards Ruby. "Is this the fella that can't read a clock?"

"Daddy," Ruby hissed. So she'd been talking about me to her father. I wondered what else she'd told him about me.

"That's me, and I deeply apologize for keeping your daughter away from you for a minute longer than she had to be." I flashed a grin at Miss Hayes, and she rolled her eyes in response.

Jack's mustache twitched in a smile. "Apology accepted, son. Raising kids by yourself isn't easy." He smiled and glanced at his daughter. She returned his smile, but there was a tinge of sadness in it.

"Hayes, table for two," the hostess called to the small crowd in the waiting area.

"Excuse me, miss," Jack called to the hostess. "Can you make that table for four? These nice folks will be joining us for dinner." He turned and addressed Nina, "If that's okay with this young lady."

"Yes." Nina nodded and was bouncing on the balls of her feet with excitement.

"Okay, give me another couple of minutes." The hostess smiled at Nina before returning to the hostess stand.

I shot a glance at Miss Hayes. The uncomfortable expression she was wearing made me think about reconsidering imposing on her family dinner. Then Nina grabbed her hand and pulled her into the dining room. She shrugged and gave me a helpless half-smile. I was helpless too.

FIVE

RUBY

I was seriously regretting agreeing to go out for dinner when Dad suggested it. Still, I didn't have the heart to tell him that it wasn't a good idea because his behavior was becoming more and more unpredictable.

He was better off in the familiar surroundings of his house, but I could understand his feelings of confinement and helplessness. So, I decided to go to Manny's. It was a less than five-minute drive from the house, and he'd been there a few times before. It felt like the safest option.

At least, I thought it was the safest option until I was sitting at a table with one of my students and her father. Nina Jones was a little girl who was slowly stealing my heart, and Spencer Jones was a man I was fighting a serious physical attraction to. It was a fight I was losing every time I looked up at him across the table to see him gazing at me.

"So, Ruby told me you recently moved here from the Midwest." Dad addressed Spencer as he waited for our food. He blinked, averting his gaze and focusing on Dad instead.

"Yes, sir. Nina and I are from Chicago." He patted the top of her head.

"So what brings you two to California?" he asked.

"Dad, don't you think you're asking a lot of questions?" I placed my hand on my father's forearm and gave it a gentle squeeze.

"No, it's okay." Spencer grinned at me, showing me the perfect smile that he usually reserved for his daughter. "I don't mind. I moved here for work. I'm a securities analyst, and I needed a job with a little more flexibility for Nina." He beamed a smile at his daughter, and my heart melted a little more.

"Daddy, what's flexibility mean?" she asked.

"It means I spend less time working and more time with you." He winked at her. She tried to wink back and ended up blinking instead. It was one of the cutest things I'd ever seen. I cracked a smile that faltered when I saw Spencer watching me with his own smile.

"I like flexibility." Nina nodded before taking a sip of her apple juice, making the entire table erupted into chuckles.

"Me too, Little Bit. So what about you, Mr. Hayes. Have you always lived here in Rancho Verde?"

"Call me Jack," he said, and Spencer nodded. "And to answer your question, yes, and I've lived in the same house for over thirty years."

Spencer turned his gaze on me again. I wrapped my hands around my water glass to keep them steady. Having an actual conversation with Spencer Jones outside of school was nerve-wracking enough, but I was also tense about Dad being out in public.

"So, how long have you been a kindergarten teacher, Miss Hayes?"

"You might as well call me Ruby," I said, taking a sip of water. I shot a quick glance at Dad. He was perfectly fine and seemed to be enjoying himself. I turned my attention back to Spencer. "This is my third year."

"So, you've lived here your entire life?" he asked.

"Yes." I nodded. "Rancho Verde is a great town. It's beautiful. The weather is great. The people are nice."

"I've only lived here for about a month, but I agree." He smiled at me again. My heart started to race, and I felt the same electric feeling followed by belly flutters whenever we locked eyes.

Luckily, at that moment, our food arrived. I'd called ahead to ask if the restaurant could accommodate Dad's diet, and I moved the salt shaker out of his reach.

We ate in silence for a few minutes before Dad spoke.

"Hey, Spencer. Would you pass me the salt?"

"Sure." Spencer reached for the shaker, and I slid it out of his reach.

"Nice try, Dad." I cut my eyes at my father and turned to Spencer. "I'm sorry. He's on a restricted low-salt diet."

"Low salt, not no salt," Dad grumbled.

"Sorry, I didn't know." Spencer's face fell, and he suddenly looked sheepish.

"It's fine." I tried to paste on a smile and salvage the mood, which was on a downward trajectory. "How's your steak?"

"Good." Spencer nodded, and I could tell Dad and I had made dinner more awkward than it already was. Dad's face was set, and he was pushing his food around his plate with his fork. He was not only angry that I wouldn't give him the salt, but he was also embarrassed. Suddenly, I felt like the villain again. I wondered if I should've just let him have a little bit of salt and not ruin our dinner, but I couldn't do that. His diet was strict for a reason. I knew this wasn't my fault, but I still felt guilty.

"How are your chicken fingers, Nina?" I asked.

"Good," she said quietly. "Why is everybody sad?" She looked around at the adults at the table.

"Nobody's sad, baby." Spencer gently tugged on one of her braids and kissed the top of her head. "We're all just quiet because we're eating."

She wasn't buying it, but she didn't question her dad.

My dad got up from the table.

"Hey, where are you going?" I asked.

"To use the men's room, if I have your permission," he snapped. I gulped and blinked back the hot tears that prickled in my eyes. I noticed Spencer's eyes flash, and I could tell he wanted to say something to my dad, perhaps to defend me, but I shot him a glance and gave my head a little shake. He sat back but didn't take his eyes off of my father.

After a deep calming breath and reminding myself that this wasn't my father speaking, I calmly asked, "Do you know the way? I can show you."

"No," he snapped again. "I can find it." He threw his napkin in his chair and stalked off in the direction of the restroom. I deflated and stared at my plate, cursing myself for letting Dad talk me into leaving the house. I felt a warm presence next to me and inhaled a puff of spicy, woodsy cologne.

"Hey, are you okay?" Spencer put his arm around my shoulders.

"Yes, I'm fine. I'm sorry. Dad's not usually like this."

"What's wrong with Mr. Jack?" Nina asked.

"He doesn't always feel good, and sometimes it makes him a little cranky," I said. Spencer still had his arm around my shoulders, and I couldn't remember the last time I'd been held or comforted like this.

"Does he have a tummy ache?" she asked, her pretty brown eyes so full of concern made my heart clench.

"Kind of like a tummy ache, but not really." I gave her a small smile.

"Do his boobies hurt, like Mommy?" Her expression switched from concern to fear.

I looked at Spencer. His face fell, and his hand dropped from my shoulder.

"No, sweetie, not like Mommy." He rushed to sit by her side and hugged her to him. Tears that I could no longer blink away fell from my eyes. This dinner was officially a disaster and couldn't get any worse.

"I'm so sorry. Maybe you should take Nina home."

"Hey, don't cry. This isn't your fault. This isn't anyone's fault. Are you going to be okay?"

"Yes, I'll be fine. I'll take care of the check and get Dad home."

"I'll take care of the check, and you just take care of your father."

We were both looking in the direction of the men's room, suddenly realizing that Dad had been gone too long. I looked at Spencer before placing my palms on the table to get to my feet.

"No, it's the men's room. I'll go. Stay with Nina."

"No, it's not your responsibility. I'll go."

"Ruby." He placed his hand over mine, covering it with a warmth that spread up my arm and through my entire body before settling in my chest. "It's fine. Let me go."

I nodded and slid in the chair next to Nina that Spencer vacated.

"Where's my daddy going?" she asked me.

"He's going to check on my dad to make sure he's okay."

"Oh." She took a deep breath and let it out. "Miss Ruby?"

"Yes, Nina?"

"Are you an angel?" she asked. I looked down at her. She had a deep brown complexion, almost as deep as her dad's with an adorable round nose and large brown eyes that looked like they'd seen the world.

She looked like an angel, and after three years of thinking I'd been asked every question by a five-year-old, Nina managed to surprise me.

"No, sweetie. I'm not an angel."

"How do you know you're not an angel?" She narrowed her eyes at me.

"Well." I chuckled. "I don't know. I mean, I could be an angel, but I think if I was an angel, I'd have wings, right?"

"Not all angels have wings," she said with a degree of certainty so high that I had to bite my lip to keep from laughing again when she was so serious.

Spencer popped up in my peripheral vision. I looked up and he shook his head. My heart started to pound. In the next moment, a man in a suit approached Spencer and whispered something in his ear. Spencer nodded and followed the man to the back of the restaurant. Five of the longest minutes went by before the suited man, who I deduced was the restaurant's manager, Spencer, and my father emerged. They walked in from the opposite direction of the restroom. Spencer shook hands with the manager and clapped him on the shoulder. My father looked sheepish, and Spencer was giving him a reassuring smile.

"You ladies ready to go?" He quickly scooped Nina into his arms, and discreetly pointed his eyes at my father's pants. Dad had wet himself, and Spencer didn't want to risk Nina noticing and mentioning it. I mouthed the words *thank you,* and we moved in the direction of the exit.

"The check." I gasped.

"I already took care of it."

I GOT DAD INTO THE CAR, WHERE WE DROVE HOME IN mostly silence except for Dad's apologies. I told him he had nothing to be sorry for and that everything would be okay, though I was only certain about one of those things.

I'd just opened the door to let Dad into the house when I saw the headlights in our driveway. A tall figure emerged from the car. The unmistakable silhouette of Spencer Jones walked towards my front door.

"I still say he's sweet on you," Daddy said before kissing me on the forehead and going inside, insisting he didn't need my help.

"You followed us home?" I asked when he was close enough to hear me.

"I wanted to make sure you got here okay," he said as he joined me on the porch. "How's Jack?"

"He's embarrassed and frustrated, but he's fine. Thank you for your help."

"You don't need to thank me. It's called basic human decency. I don't want you to applaud me for doing what I should be doing anyway." He smirked at me, and my lips involuntarily curled into a smile.

"You have a beautiful smile." His eyes raked over my face, drinking in every detail. My smile grew wider at his words, and he took a step closer.

"So do you." I swallowed. Spencer took another step closer and reached out, grazing my hips with his fingertips before bracketing my waist with his palms, pulling me closer. "What about Nina?"

"Nina is asleep," he whispered with his lips inches from mine.

"I really want to kiss you," I whispered.

"That's a relief," Spencer said, "or this would be really awkward." He tightened his grip on my hips.

A small chuckle bubbled from my lips.

"We shouldn't do this. You're my favorite student's dad."

"We definitely should… Wait, Nina's your favorite student. I thought teachers were supposed to love all of their students equally." Our lips were almost touching.

"That's just some bullshit that teachers say," I whispered. Spencer smiled before pressing our lips together.

SIX

SPENCER

"So then what happened?" Simi asked.

"Well, we made out on her porch like a couple of horny virgins. Then I went home, put Nina to bed, took a shower"—*where I jerked off until I nearly passed out*—"and then I went to bed."

"And how long ago was this?"

"A week ago." I sighed.

"So what have you been doing since then."

"Nothing. Same old shit. I pick up Nina from school and Ruby doesn't mention it. It's like she's pretending it didn't happen."

"Ouch, little brother. I didn't realize you were that bad at kissing." Simi laughed.

"I'm not bad at kissing. It was a weird night. I wish she would talk to me about it."

"Are you ready for what she might say?"

"What do you mean?"

"I mean, maybe she's not ready. It seems like she's got a lot to deal with, and getting involved with one of her students' parents is not the move. She had an emotional night and got carried away. It happens to the best of us. Did you ever think that she wears that wedding ring so that she doesn't get hit on by the parents of her students?"

"You make me sound like a creep. You weren't there. The feelings were definitely mutual. She said she wanted to kiss me and then she kissed me. She kissed the hell out of me."

"Listen, Spence, I don't want you to get your hopes up."

Ruby got a lot more than my hopes up that night. That kiss awakened parts of me that I thought had died with Sarai. Seeing the way she cared for her father, all by herself, made me fear for her and respect her even more than I already did. Even when dinner got stressful, she remained calm and focused. She even checked in on Nina.

Yes, she was beautiful. Yes, she was sexy, and yes, her kisses were softer and sweeter than I had been imagining for the last few weeks, but Ruby Hayes was so much more than a pretty face and a pair of soft bee-stung lips. I wanted to make it my mission to get to know those other parts of her. I wanted her to trust me with her burdens, share her smiles, and anything else she was willing to give me.

"I think it's too late for that," I muttered.

"Shit."

"What?"

"Speaking of getting hopes up…" She paused. "Mom has seen the photos of Nina's necklaces." Simi was burying the lede and trying to deflect responsibility for the shit storm she'd kicked up. She showed Mom pictures of Ruby and me gazing into each other's eyes like two star-crossed lovers.

"And?"

"She may have gotten a little excited. She's asking a lot of questions."

"And what did you say?"

"What could I say? I don't know anything."

I groaned, knowing it would be only a matter of time before I would be getting a call from my mother, demanding details about Ruby that I wasn't prepared to give.

"All right, sis. Let me get to work."

"Don't be mad. Mommy wanted to see pictures of Nina's necklaces. Did she see the display photos?"

"Yes, she's been telling all her friends that she is a jewelry designer like her aunt, and her necklaces cost a hundred dollars, but you can only buy them in Chicago." I started chuckling when I heard Simi cackling on the other end of the phone.

"Stop. Are you serious? That girl is too much." She was trying to talk between fits of laughter. "I can't wait to come visit you two. Go do your important work, little brother. I love you."

"Love you too, sis."

I put my phone on vibrate and headed in my first meeting of the day.

"WHAT'S HER NAME?" MY MOM ASKED.

"I'm afraid to tell you," I said while rocking in my office chair. I rushed through my meetings and was organizing the stacks of paper on my desk to decide which pressing client files I needed to take home tonight. It was a quarter after two, and if I could get Mom off the phone in the next twenty minutes, I would make it to Nina's school on time.

"Why? I'm just going to do an internet search for her and check her social medias."

Jesus Christ.

"That's why, Ma. There's nothing to tell. It was just a picture, and I don't want you cyberstalking Nina's teacher."

"I wouldn't be cyberstalking her. I just want to know more about her. Where did she go to school? Where are her people from? You should want to know these things too if she's taking care of your daughter all day."

"Ma, you're not fooling anybody." I chuckled as I slid the last of my files into my messenger bag.

"Okay, fine." She let out an exasperated huff. "She is a pretty girl, and Nina seems to like her a lot. She's single, and so are you. You need to move on, and Nina needs a strong female figure in her life. She had plenty before you snatched her up and moved halfway across the country. "

I rolled my eyes and sank into my chair. My mother made it sound like I'd kidnapped Nina. Lord knows she laid plenty of guilt trips on me when I was considering this move. I left my friends, and Nina and I left our family behind, which included Sarai's parents, who I thought about constantly. They were supportive of the move, and though Nina and I talk to them at least once a week, I know it must hurt to have this last piece of their daughter so far away.

"Mom. You're reading too much into a picture. I'm not ready to move on, and we're just getting settled in a new life."

"You're not reading enough into that picture. Don't block your blessings, baby," she said. "Remember, this is what Sarai wanted for you and Nina."

"Yes, I remember. Of course, I remember."

When Sarai was first diagnosed, she decided to make a video diary of what she called her journey with breast cancer. Once her diagnosis became terminal, she turned the project into videos for Nina and me, things she would want us to know when she was gone. There were videos about friendships, women stuff that I wouldn't be able to help Nina with, and God help me, dating advice for me.

Those were the hardest to watch. I was watching the woman I was supposed to grow old with telling me how to move on without her. It was also how I found out that she hated the sweater vests I used to wear when we were first dating. I didn't watch them after she died, but Nina was obsessed with them.

"Ma, that doesn't mean I'm supposed to start dating the first woman I met." But Ruby wasn't the first woman I'd met. There were plenty of women who tried to get close to me after Sarai's death. Some of them used Nina to do it, but none of them ever came close the way Ruby did. I wasn't about to explain any of this to my mother.

"I'm only saying, baby, I want to see you and Nina settled. You're a good-looking man, employed, and my grandbaby is a special little girl. If you're going to live on the other side of the country, I want to know you're happy."

"We'll get there, Ma. We need time."

"My offer is still good to fly out there and stay with you. Help you get settled."

God, no.

"Thank you, Ma. That won't be necessary, and what would Dad do without you?" I chuckled.

"I love you, baby," my mom said in a sigh.

"I know, Ma, I—" I was interrupted by a knock on my door. Jason poked his head in before I could tell him to come in. His face was filled with panic and paler than usual.

"Shit. I was hoping you left." He groaned. I looked at the clock. It was almost three o'clock. I was going to be late picking up Nina. "Don't leave your office. Stay quiet. We're on lockdown. Some lunatic with a gun got past security and is roaming the halls."

What the fuck?

"Hey, Ma." I tried to keep my voice calm, hoping she didn't hear what Jason said. "Something came up at work. I have to let you go."

"Okay, baby. Call me later." She sighed, and it gave me a small measure of comfort that she didn't sound worried.

"I will. Ma, I love you."

SEVEN

RUBY

Three forty-five found Nina and me in the middle of an alphabet matching game when my classroom phone rang.

"Hello, room ten, Ruby Hayes speaking."

"Ruby, thank God. It's Spencer." Something in the tone of his voice made my heart race. He'd never called the school to let us know he was running late.

"Hi, Spencer. Is everything okay?"

"No, wheres Nina? Is she okay? Can I talk to her?" There was panic mounting in his voice, making my chest clench and arms prickle with goose bumps.

"Yes, of course. Hold on." I held the phone away from my ear. "Nina, your dad is on the phone."

She shot me a confused expression, mirroring my own inner confusion before she ran over to the phone. I handed her the receiver.

"Hi, Daddy!" she chirped. "Are you on your way to come to get me?" She paused, listening to her father's response.

"Why not?" Another pause. Nina shot me a glance and smiled.

"Okay. See you later, Daddy. Love you too." She smiled and handed me the phone.

"Spencer, what's going on?" I asked.

"I need you to do me a favor." His tone was grave, and the volume of his voice was barely above a whisper.

"Of course," I answered without thinking. "Anything."

"I need you to watch Nina for a while."

"What? A while? How long is a while?"

"I don't know. Hopefully not longer than a few hours."

"What is going on?"

"I'll tell you, but you have to promise to stay calm and don't scare Nina." His voice got lower.

"Okay." I took a deep breath, smiled at Nina, who had resumed playing with the letter cards, then turned my back to her, bracing myself for what Spencer was about to tell me.

"My office is on lockdown."

I cleared my throat to cover the small, strangled cry I let out. I knew precisely what lockdown meant. In my first year of teaching, we had two active shooter drills. The next year we had six drills. This year we were doing them every month.

"Are you okay?" Hot, sharp tears were springing into my eyes, and I felt the hand holding the phone's receiver begin to shake.

"I'm fine. I'm hiding in a closet. I don't think the shooter is on my floor, and I've been communicating with law enforcement. They know where I am." Spencer's voice was less panicked than before and more reassuring, making me wonder if he was trying to calm me down. Then I wondered if he was downplaying the amount of danger he was in for my benefit.

"Are you supposed to be on your phone?"

"Not really, but I wanted to talk to Nina, and I wanted to hear your voice." He sighed.

My heart clenched at his words. A week ago, Spencer and I had the dinner from Hell, where he rescued my father from a potentially embarrassing situation with such generosity and grace. Then he wrapped me in his arms on my porch and kissed me senseless.

I hadn't stopped thinking about that night. His embrace was strong but so gentle. His lips were firm as they commanded me to open myself to him, and I did. In his arms, all the stress about my job, my father, and my financial troubles melted away, and I was only his. Our bodies molded together as if God made me fit in the palms of Spencer Jones' hands.

In the week that followed, I'd kept him at arm's length. Nothing that felt that good could last, and I didn't have the strength to nurse a broken heart on top of everything else.

Now, Spencer was hiding in a closet, not knowing if he would live or die, and all he wanted was to hear my voice. The tears that were pooling in my eyes began to flow down my cheeks.

"Ruby?" Spencer called.

"Yes?" I croaked in a small whisper.

"Please don't cry. I need you to do something else for me."

"Okay."

"My sister's name is Simi Jones. She has a jewelry store called Simi- Precious in Chicago. S-I-M-I. If something happens to me—"

"Spencer," I interrupted him. "No. Don't talk like that."

"Ruby, please. If something happens to me, I need you to contact her."

"You can contact her yourself when you get home."

"Listen, I don't want my family to worry. They're in Chicago. There's nothing they can do," he pleaded. "Please, promise me you'll do that for me."

"Yes," I whispered finally, "but you're going to be fine."

"Listen, I need your number."

"My number?"

"Yeah, I'm gonna write it on my arm, in case…"

I wanted to argue that he didn't need to do that, but if it made him feel better, I would. It also felt strange that after everything we'd been through, we didn't have each other's numbers. I recited the digits.

"Wow. After all these weeks, it took an active shooter for me to get your number." He chuckled.

"Are you seriously cracking jokes right now?" I smiled, and two more tears streaked down my cheeks. I wiped them away and glanced at Nina.

"Are you smiling right now?" he asked.

"Yes," I answered.

"I can hear it." He paused for a minute. "Listen, Ruby, I should preserve my battery. I'll call you as soon as I can. Take care of my baby for me…and Nina, too." He laughed.

"You are too much, Spencer Jones." I huffed out an exasperated chuckle. My heart leaped at his little declaration, even if it was disguised as a joke. He wanted me to know how he felt about me.

"I guess near-death experiences make me reckless." He sighed. "I'll talk to you soon, beautiful."

"I'll *see* you soon," I said. "Please be safe."

MY PRINCIPAL CONFIRMED THAT SPENCER HAD GIVEN her permission to release Nina to me. She asked if there was something she should know about my relationship with the Joneses. I told her that they were new in town, didn't have any friends, and Nina had sort of bonded with me. All of this was true, but I left out the part about Spencer doing things with his tongue that kept me up late thinking about what else he could do with that tongue in other places on my body.

I BORROWED A BOOSTER SEAT FROM THE SCHOOL AND brought Nina to my house, where thankfully, Dad was in good spirits. I'm sure Nina's presence helped. He sat through four episodes of the Super Hero Girls, while Nina talked animatedly about all of the characters. It had been over two decades since I was Nina's age, but Dad didn't miss a beat with her.

I started to make dinner, and he joined me in the kitchen.

"So, I saw on the news that some fella was shooting up an office building downtown." He took a tomato out of the bowl of vegetables and started chopping it. My eyes began to sting and well with tears. His brow furrowed.

"Onion," I croaked and held up the purple and white onion I'd been slicing.

"Ruby? I was born during the day, but it wasn't yesterday." My dad pursed his lips, and his head dropped to the side.

"Yes," I confessed. "It's Spencer's office. I talked to him. He said he's safe and hidden, but that was four hours ago." My voice started to tremble. My phone buzzed on the kitchen table, and we both jumped. I dove for it, turning it over to see the caller ID. It was Sabrina.

"Hey, girl. I can't talk right now."

"Have you been watching the news? Spencer's office building is on lockdown. There's a shooter. Have you —" My best friend must have resumed her internet sleuthing after drinks a couple weeks ago.

"Brina, I know. I haven't been watching because Nina's here with me." I should've gotten off the phone, but I was desperate for any news. "What are they saying on TV?"

"There are no confirmed shootings, but there are hostages. They're sending in a hostage negotiator. Have you talked to him?"

"A few hours ago. Spencer said he was hiding, and he wasn't sure which floor the shooter was on." My voice began to tremble, and I could feel tears springing to my eyes. I wanted to tell Brina to come over so she could hold my hand and watch me cry while we waited for news, but I couldn't do that. Nina had to be my first priority.

"I'm sure he's fine." Her voice was an attempt at the reassurance she knew I needed.

"Yeah," I responded with half a heart. "Brina, I have to go. I don't want to upset Nina, but I'll call you as soon as I know anything."

"Okay. Talk to you soon. Love you."

"Love you too."

During dinner, Nina talked a blue streak, and it was a welcome respite from the feeling of impending dread that was threatening to suffocate me as the minutes dragged on. Dad didn't complain about the food being bland and even ate half of his salad to encourage Nina to eat hers. It didn't work, but I applauded his effort. For a brief moment, I thought it would be nice to eat dinner with Nina more often, then I remembered why she was eating dinner with us and my heart clenched again.

After dinner, Nina informed me that it was Wednesday, and on Wednesdays, her dad washed and braided her hair. I ran her a bubble bath—with extra bubbles at her insistence—washed her hair with my shampoo, rinsed and added conditioner before piling the slippery locks on top of her head with a hair tie. I soaped up a washcloth and let her wash, helping her with the bits she didn't do well enough or couldn't reach. After undoing her hair, I began to work through the tangles with my fingers and my wide-toothed comb.

"Daddy always rinses my hair before he combs it," she said. *Ouch. Seriously, Spencer?* "I like it better the way you do it. It doesn't hurt as much."

"I'll be sure and tell your daddy that when he comes to get you."

"Thank. You." She said in two exaggerated sighs of relief, that made me giggle. "When is my daddy coming? He's never been this late before."

Showtime, Ruby. Nina was a smart little girl, and I couldn't betray an ounce of the fear and panic I was feeling. I pasted on a big smile.

"I don't know, sweetie, but I know he got stuck at work, and he's gonna come get you as soon as he can. Okay?"

"Okay." She seemed to be happy with that explanation. "Miss Ruby?"

"Yes, Nina?"

"Can you do my hair different? Daddy only knows how to do two braids. It's kinda boring." She told me this like she was telling me the weather, and I had to roll my lips between my teeth to keep from laughing again.

"Okay. Let's see what we can do."

AFTER BATHTIME, I TUCKED NINA INTO MY BED, wearing one of my t-shirts, where I read her favorite book *Where the Wild Things Are*, which also happened to be my favorite book when I was her age. She asked to wear one of my sleep bonnets so she wouldn't mess up her new hairstyle. I smiled at her tiny form as she drifted off to sleep, wondering how someone could simultaneously be five and thirty-five years old.

Downstairs, I poured myself a glass of wine and curled up on the couch to wait for Spencer—*or the police*, a tiny voice in my head called. I pulled out a stack of lesson plans to distract me, but I couldn't focus. Dad sat with me for a while, but after a couple of hours, he went to bed.

I was on my second glass when I heard the knock. My heart sank. I was sure Spencer would call us when he was on his way. I took a deep breath, steeled myself, and walked to the door.

EIGHT

SPENCER

The door opened, and one of the two people I was desperate to lay eyes on flung herself into my arms. I'd been sitting in a closet for seven hours. Then I sat in the back of an ambulance wrapped in a blanket while being questioned by police. I must have smelled like death, but she didn't seem to care. She smelled like heaven: flowers, berries, and the faint smell of chocolate that I knew must have been cocoa butter.

"Oh, thank God." Her eyes were filled with tears when she pulled away from me. I wiped them away by brushing the pads of my thumbs across her soft skin, right before she punched me in the chest. "Why didn't you call me and tell me you were okay?"

I pulled my cell out of my pocket to show her.

"My phone died," I said deadpan. "Do you have a charger I can borrow?" I grinned at her, and she narrowed her eyes at me, smirked, and punched me in the chest again. "Where's Nina?"

"She's asleep in my room. Do you want to see her?"

My smile faded as the magnitude of how this day could have ended crashed over me like a tidal wave. Nina could have lost me. In the last conversations I had with my mother and sister, I was fussing at them about a picture of me and the woman I pretended I wasn't falling in love with. That same woman would have had to call them and tell them I was gone. I tried to stay calm during my phone call with Ruby because I didn't want to worry her any more than she had to be, but I was terrified.

I nodded at Ruby, unable to form words, and she led me to her bedroom. I walked in and crouched beside my daughter's sleeping form. She was wearing an oversized t-shirt and a pale purple bonnet that made her look like the old lady from a Looney Tunes cartoon. Simi wears them to bed, too, and I wondered if I'd missed some unspoken rule about raising little girls that Simi and Ruby knew. I crawled into bed next to her and pulled her into me, kissing her forehead. Nina stirred.

"Hi, Daddy," she whispered in a sleepy voice.

"Hey, Little Bit," I whispered. "Are you okay?"

"I'm fine." She yawned. "I'm really sleepy, Daddy. Can we talk in the morning?"

I shot Ruby a look of incredulity, and she shrugged. Her eyes were sparkling like she was lit from within, and she was trying not to laugh.

"We have to get up and go home, baby. Miss Ruby needs her room back so she can go to bed."

Nina groaned in response.

"Spencer," Ruby whispered. "If you want, you can sleep in here with Nina. I was planning to sleep in the guest room downstairs."

"Yes, we'll do that," Nina replied.

"I couldn't put you out like that," I said. To be honest, I was physically, emotionally, and mentally drained. I must have made the drive to Ruby's house on desperation and adrenaline, but once I got to hold my girls in my arms, the exhaustion set in.

"It's okay. I insist." She smiled at me. "I can find you some of my father's pajamas. They may look a little young on you because you're bigger than Dad. We have some spare toothbrushes. You can take a shower…"

Ah, she did notice the smell.

I grinned at her and nodded.

"Are we staying here tonight?" Nina asked.

"Yes, sweetie. We're staying," I told her.

"Good," she groaned before rolling over and closing her eyes.

I looked at Ruby, shaking my head. She had a hand clapped over her mouth, and her shoulders were shaking with laughter.

RUBY WASN'T JOKING ABOUT HER DAD'S PAJAMAS. FROM the waist up, I looked like a male model. From the waist down, I looked like Steve Urkel. The shower was energizing, so instead of going to sleep, I checked on Nina again and then went downstairs to find Ruby.

She was sitting on the couch in pajamas, twirling a wine glass between her thumb and forefinger.

"Hey, you," I called to her. "Got any more of that?"

She turned to look at me, and her eyes went wide with shock before she tucked her bottom lip between her teeth and bit down, grinning. She put the wine glass on the table.

"How do I look?" I did a turn for her. She burst out laughing.

"Umm, like I shouldn't make you angry." She grinned. I leaned down, put one knee on the couch beside her. Then I wrapped my arms around her waist and crawled on top of her.

"You wouldn't like me when I'm angry," I whispered with my lips inches from hers.

"Are you sure about that?" she whispered back. My pajamas got tighter, and I knew she felt it because she grinned at me.

"Ruby—" I began.

"I know. You care about me. I care about you. We both love Nina. You almost died today, and now you want to have sex?" She raised her eyebrows.

"Um, pretty much. I planned on being smoother than that, but that about covers it." I chuckled.

"Me, too." She dragged her fingernails over my scalp before she wrapped her fingers around my head and pulled me down for a kiss. Ruby pressed our bodies together and wrapped her legs around my waist as we tasted each other for the first time in seven damn days. After what I went through today, going that long without kissing her again wasn't an option. I separated our lips.

"I don't just want to have sex," I said. "I want you. I want to be with you."

I searched her eyes, looking for a response to my words. She seemed to deflate, and she sunk into the couch below me, slowly uncoiling herself from my body.

"I don't wanna get hurt. I know that's a stupid thing to say because it's something I'd have no control over, but I just have too much on my plate right now."

"Maybe you need someone to grab a fork and help you."

She giggled.

"Did you just think of that?" she asked. I nodded, and she smiled. "Corny."

"What? That metaphor was perfect." I reached down and tickled her.

"Can we take it slow?" She bit her lip and looked up at me, her brows knitted together.

"Sure. Of course." I started to back away from her on the couch. She grabbed the collar of my t-shirt and pulled me on top of her.

"No, we should definitely have sex tonight." She kissed me. "I meant, let's not rush to put a label on this. Let's just spend time together and see what feels right."

"Okay." I nodded. "I can handle that, but to be clear: we are having sex tonight?"

"Oh, absolutely."

"GOT 'EM." RUBY CLOSED AND LOCKED THE DOOR TO the guest room before holding up the strip of condoms. "I had to sneak past Nina to grab them out of my nightstand. They'd been in there for years. I had to check the expiration date." She giggled.

"Then, what are you doing all the way over there?" I stood up and walked towards her, with my arms held out. "Come here."

She stepped forward, and I wrapped my arms around her waist.

"I thought I was never gonna see you again," I whispered as I dragged my nose over her shoulder, inhaling her delicious scent. "I couldn't stop thinking about that kiss."

"Me, neither." She panted. "I'm so glad you're okay." She wrapped her arms around my neck and pulled our bodies closer. I began ghosting kisses over the curve of her chin before settling on her soft lips and covering them with my own. She let out a little moan that vibrated in my chest, before parting her lips to grant me entrance to her luscious mouth. Ruby tasted like red wine, sweetness, and months of answered prayers.

I scooped her under the thighs and carried her to a nearby desk, setting her on top.

I slid my fingertips over the soft, smooth skin of her waist as I gripped the hem of her pajama top and pulled it over her head. She wasn't wearing a bra underneath, and her breasts were small, perky—just the size of the palm of my hand—with large dark brown nipples. I couldn't stop myself from leaning forward, sucking one into my mouth and gently applying pressure with my teeth.

"Hmmm," she moaned. Ruby was raking her nails over my scalp again. I worshipped her body, making my way down her waist and across her small rounded belly that again seemed to be made just for me to hold. She wiggled her hips as I helped her out of her pajama bottoms and panties. My hand slid between our bodies as I kissed her soft lips again. I parted her slick curls with my finger sliding over the hood of her clit, making her yelp. She was wet with arousal, ready for me to taste her. I began to kiss a trail down her torso.

"Spencer, what are you doing?" she moaned.

"Everything." I was almost to my knees when I looked up at her with raised eyebrows. "Is that okay with you?"

"Yeah." She grinned, placing a hand on top of my head.

"Don't mess up my waves," I teased.

"I can't promise that," she said with a giggle that was cut short by me, smoothing my tongue over her clit. I slid one of her thighs over my shoulder and continued to taste her. She was fucking delicious. Ruby Hayes continued to exceed my expectations. Long lonely nights with my hands wrapped around my dick did nothing to prepare me for the reality of this goddess: the smell of her sex, her smooth, soft skin caressing me as she writhed and squirmed with my hands gripping her waist to steady her. "Oooh, Spencer. Oh my God, Spencer."

"Shhh." I planted a kiss on her inner thigh. "You'll wake the whole house."

"I can't help it," she panted as I slid a finger into her, then two. It was a tight fit, and I was trying not to imagine how good it would feel when Ruby's heat was gripping my shaft. I needed to feel her warm, soft body wrapped around mine, but I needed her to come first. Ruby felt and tasted too good. I was living on borrowed time, and I wouldn't last much longer without being inside her. I twisted my fingers in her, moving my fingertips over the tight patch of skin, deep inside her.

"Whoa," she breathed. "Keep doing that."

I looked up at Ruby. Her head was thrown back, exposing her lovely throat, and she was gripping the edge of the desk. Her chest was heaving. One glistening bead of sweat cascaded between her breasts. I leaned forward and caught it with my tongue before it reached her navel.

"Fuck, Ruby. I need you." I groaned, pumping my fingers in and out of her, brushing her sensitive pearl with my thumb. "I need you right now." I moved my thumb to cover her swollen clit with my lips and began to suck while teasing the tip with my tongue.

"Then, take me, Spencer," she whined as she began to come apart in my hands. "I'm yours. Take me."

When Ruby's spasming subsided, I stood and pulled my fingers out of her and sucked them into my mouth while she ripped a condom from the strip, pulled down my pants, rolled it over my dick, and guided me into her.

She grabbed the sides of my face and gazed at me as I slowly slid into her. My Ruby felt so good. She felt too good. I haven't been with anyone like this since Sarai's diagnosis. I never imagined feeling like this for anyone else.

"Spencer," Ruby called to me, and my eyes met hers. "Look at me. I want you to see me when we make love."

"Yes," I whispered. I forced my eyes open to gaze into her chestnut-hued irises, flecked with gold. Her pupils were dilated. Thick onyx-colored lashes framed the eyes that were gazing back at me with so much passion and intensity that it was overwhelming. I tucked my bottom lip in between my teeth and bit down, trying not to explode into her.

"Do you see me?" she asked. Her glittering brown eyes were searching mine for something. Was it reassurance or recognition?

Admittedly, I felt guilty when I first realized my attraction to Ruby. I'd already found the love of my life. We'd made vows. We created a life together, both figuratively and literally. Now, she was gone. I knew her last wish was for me to move on, but I wasn't sure I could just cast my love for her aside for someone new.

Then I met Ruby Hayes, and as my feelings for her grew, I realized that I didn't have to cast my love for Sarai aside. There was room in my heart for them both. I would always love Sarai for all of the things she taught me about myself and the wonderful but short time we had, but I could love Ruby too. I desperately wanted to love Ruby if she would give me the chance.

"Yes, Ruby. I see you. I only see you." My eyes filled with tears at the declaration, and it felt like a weight had been lifted. I had gone from almost losing everything I loved tonight to finding everything I needed in Ruby's eyes.

She wrapped her arms around my neck and her legs around my waist, drawing me deeper into her until she was full.

"Oh, Spencer. You feel so good," she moaned as I slid in and out of her, gripping her thighs while trying to make this moment last as long as I could. Ruby's slick heat was gripping me, squeezing me as I buried myself in her. The sharp points of her nails dug into my back, and she embraced me, trying to merge our bodies into one. She arched her back, pressing the globes of her small breasts into my chest. "Oh, yes, Spencer. Right there. That feels so fucking good."

Her words were driving me over the edge, and I was ready to crash. I reached between our bodies again, finding her clit with my thumb and massaging.

"Come for me, baby. Come for me again," I rasped into her neck between kisses as I thrust my hips into hers. Ruby granted my request in loud moans that I had to stifle with hungry kisses, and I followed her, hugging her close to me as I clenched and relaxed.

WE MOVED TO THE BED WHERE WE KEPT REACHING for each other until half the condoms were gone.

"That was incredible." She planted a kiss on my chest and started giggling.

"I know. I have to escape the icy clutches of death more often."

"Stop." She slapped my chest. "That's not funny."

"I'm sorry, baby." I kissed her curls.

"Did you just call me baby?" She hit me with a lazy, sexy grin that made me want to reach for her again.

"I called you baby this afternoon."

"That's right. You did," Ruby recalled. "God, that feels like a hundred years ago."

"I feel like I aged a hundred years in that closet."

"So, what happened? If you're okay to talk about it."

"Sure. Some guy's retirement account was handled by the firm. His employer mismanaged the funds, and he blamed us, well, not me but my company."

"Was anyone hurt?" she whispered.

"Yeah." I paused for a long moment and hugged her closer, not wanting to think about it, not at that moment, at least. "I was never in any real danger. He was on a different floor, but they wanted everyone to stay put just in case. I thought about making a break for it so many times, but I couldn't risk it."

"I'm glad you didn't. You did the right thing. You came back to us." She squeezed me. "Nina had a great time. She had no idea."

"Thanks again for taking care of her, and thanks for doing her hair."

"Of course." She smiled. "But Nina asked me to give you some hair tips."

"Oh yeah? She doesn't like the way I do her hair? I watched the same YouTube video thirty times to learn how to do those braids." I even bought one of those giant doll heads to practice after she went to bed.

"And they're great, but I think Nina would appreciate a little variety. And in the future, you should detangle her hair before you rinse the conditioner out. The tangles come out more easily, and it's less painful for her—and you, probably." She smiled and kissed my chest.

"Really?" I picked my head up to look at her. "Why didn't she ever say anything?"

"I think she didn't want to hurt your feelings." She gave me a tender half-smile before planting another soft kiss on my chest.

I leaned back on my pillow, wondering how long my daughter was sparing my feelings while I was torturing her.

"Thank you for telling me, Ruby."

"Of course," she replied.

"Thank you for everything you've done for us. You've been a godsend." Heaven sent, really.

"You're not exactly slacking in the helping-Ruby department, especially Nina. She's like the Jack Hayes whisperer." She laughed before giving me the full rundown of everything Nina and Jack did while they were here, including the Super Hero Girls marathon and dinnertime. "I wish she could help me persuade Dad to try an assisted living community."

"Maybe there's a way she can?"

"What do you mean?"

"We work with some nonprofits, and there's one called The Bridge that brings school-aged children to retirement communities to hang out with the residents."

"Hmmm," she mused. "That might work. There are a few moving pieces that I think I could make fit, but it's worth a shot. Thank you."

"Anything for you." I smoothed my palm over her body and settled on her hip.

"So, what are you going to do?"

"Make love to you for as long as you'll let me."

"That sounds nice, but I mean with work."

"Oh, well, the office is closed for a few days, so I guess I'll be on time picking up Nina." I tickled her.

Ruby laughed. "You'd still be late. But why don't you take her to Chicago for a few days?"

I picked my head up to look at her.

"Ruby, we kissed, and you spent a week pretending it didn't happen. Now, we have sex, and you're sending me halfway across the country. Is there something I should know?"

"No, silly." She rolled on top of me and stacked her forearms on my chest to use it as a chin rest. "You had a very traumatic experience, and I know Nina misses her family. Were you planning on telling them what happened over the phone and not in person where they can squeeze you, kiss you, and see with their own eyes that you're okay?"

Her words made perfect sense. They made so much sense that I was a little mad I didn't think of it. I loved her a little bit more, and I'd be sure to tell my mother that she had Ruby to thank for our surprise visit.

"Come with us?" I pushed a curl away from her face.

"That, sir, is the opposite of taking it slow. Plus, I have to work. But"—she leaned forward and kissed me—"I will miss you and Nina so much."

"We'll miss you too."

NINE

RUBY

"Hey, where are you going?" Spencer whispered to me as I tried to slide out of bed.

"You know where I'm going," I whispered to him while I was feeling around the floor for my bra.

"But it's so early," he said in his cute pouty voice that melted me nearly every time.

"That's the point." I was sliding into my panties. For the last three weeks, I've been coming to Spencer and Nina's house after Nina went to bed and leaving before she woke up in the morning. Occasionally, we'd have family dinner with the four of us, and we'd do fun things on the weekends, like driving to the beach or going to the drive-in. Though, we agreed—

mostly, I insisted—that Nina wasn't ready to see me sleeping over. Spencer went along with it, though I could tell he was ready for more.

I couldn't imagine my life without Nina and Spencer in it, but I was still scared, and I was glad Spencer was so patient.

"Baby," he called to me in his deep voice, "stay for a little while longer." He patted the space in his bed that I'd vacated.

"No, I can't be late today, and you better not be late either."

"Please, baby, baby, please." He shot me a puppy dog look. "You know I almost died, right?"

I snorted laughter. "That only worked once, and that was over a month ago."

"Damn." He snapped his fingers before he leaned back and locked his hands behind his head before shooting me a grin.

I buttoned up my shirt, pulled my bonnet off my head, and gave my hair a quick fluff with my fingers in the mirror before grabbing my shoes and pulling the bedroom door open.

"See you later, handsome." I blew him a kiss.

"See you later, gorgeous." He reached up and caught my kiss in his fist.

"Okay, everyone pair up and hold your buddy's hand." I was struggling to be heard over the din of squealing and giggling five- and six-year-olds. I pulled a flashlight out of my tote bag and aimed it at the ceiling of the school bus, flashing it on and off three times: the signal to be quiet and pay attention.

When I finally had twenty pairs of little eyes on me, I repeated my request along with additional instructions. Each student was paired with a classmate as a buddy. My co-teacher, Annette, and I were assisted by five parental chaperones. Each chaperone was assigned to four kids.

"Daddy, will you be my chaperone?" Nina said in a stage whisper.

"Of course," Spencer nodded at her before shooting me a grin I had to pretend to ignore. There were already rumors flying about our possible romantic involvement. We just had to make it to the end of the school year. Nina wouldn't be my student anymore, and I'd be free to date her incredibly sexy dad.

We filed off of the bus at the Seven Palms Retirement Village, where we were met by Susan, the activities director.

"Well, hello!" she called excitedly. "Look at all these smiling faces. Are you ready to make some birdhouses with some of our residents and sing songs and have a dance party?"

Susan received resounding choruses of *yeah!* after every activity she listed. I looked at my watch and began to glance around. Spencer tapped me on the shoulder and pointed to my left. My face spread into a wide grin when I saw my father and Sabrina walking towards us.

"Hey, you two," I called.

"Mister Jack," Nina squealed and ran in Dad's direction, wrapping her arms around his legs.

"Hey, little lady." Dad patted her head.

"We're here on a field trip. We're making birdhouses. Are you gonna make birdhouses with us?"

"Hold on, Nina." Spencer chuckled. "Let Mister Jack take a breath."

"Hi, Miss Sabrina." Nina smiled at Brina. They met two weeks ago when we went to the beach. "I love that dress."

"Why, thank you, Nina." Brina did a twirl before shooting me a silly look. "One of my clients made this for me. I bet if I ask them nicely, they can make one in your size. Would you like that?"

Nina bobbed her head excitedly. Those two became fast friends.

After Sabrina and Dad showed Susan their visitor's passes, they joined our crowd and headed to the recreation center where we were joined by Aunt Anita.

A dozen volunteers from The Bridge program began pairing residents and kids before teaching us to assemble and paint birdhouses. Once I checked on my students, I joined the table with Nina, Sabrina, Spencer, Daddy, and Aunt Anita.

Brina shot me a thumbs-up, so things were going well.

"So, Auntie, how do you like it here?" I asked. I could've been more subtle, but I only had a few minutes before I had to make my rounds again.

"Oh, I love it. Everyone is really nice. The food is good. There's a lot of things to do." She waved a perfectly manicured hand around, smiling. "I'm making lots of new friends."

Brina shot me a look and raised her eyebrows. I stifled a giggle. As if on cue, an older man with light brown skin and a badly dyed inky-black mustache wearing a fedora walked past our table.

"Como esta, Anita?" The man slowed his gait as he passed our table.

"Muy bien. ¿Y tu, Miguel?" Anita smiled pleasantly at Miguel and gave him a small wave.

"Muy bien. Muy bien." Miguel nodded at everyone sitting at the table. His gaze lingered on my father for a second, and Dad narrowed his eyes slightly.

"Who was that?" Daddy asked. I definitely detected a tone in his voice. Spencer and Brina noticed it too.

"Oh, that's just Miguel. One of the other residents."

"Hmm." My dad huffed before looking around and saying, "So what other stuff do they have around this place?"

Brina and I shot each other what must have been the same confused glance because Spencer laughed at us. Nina was completely oblivious, happily painting her birdhouse.

"I'll be right back." I slid off of the bench to stand.

I did a quick but not too quick walk around the rec center, checking on my students and snapping photos for the bulletin board before scooting on the bench next to Brina.

"What did I miss?" I asked her.

"A. Lot," she whispered, and she looked annoyed. Someone who didn't know Brina wouldn't be able to tell, but I knew.

"So, you don't have a roommate," Dad said to Aunt Anita.

Roommate? What the hell?

"No, Jackson," she answered, "and it would be nice to have a familiar face around. I checked when Sabrina called me, and there is a two-bedroom suite available. I know insurance covers a portion of the rent, but it would make the rest more affordable if we shared the cost."

Jackson?

Aunt Anita slid her hand into Dad's, and Dad started rubbing the pad of his thumb over the back of her wrist. I looked at Brina again. She raised her eyebrows and pursed her lips.

"I don't know, Nita..." Dad said in a sigh.

Nita? What in the entire hell?

Spencer pulled out his phone, and his thumbs started flying over the screen.

What the hell was so important that he needed to be on his phone now of all times?

I found out when my phone vibrated in my pocket.

TEACHER'S PET: ABOUT A YEAR AFTER YOUR MOM PASSED AWAY, YOUR DAD & ANITA STARTED HOOKING UP BUT DIDN'T KEEP THE RELATIONSHIP GOING BECAUSE THEY DIDN'T WANT TO RISK HURTING YOU & SABRINA.

My jaw dropped. I really did miss a lot when I went to check on my students. I tilted my phone to show

Spencer's message to Brina. Her face was a mask, which I knew after twenty years of friendship meant she was processing this new information and probably inwardly losing her shit. She glanced at my phone, read the message, and nodded.

Dad sacrificed a chance at love after Mom died because he wanted to spare my feelings and wasted over twenty years with the possible love of his life living four streets away.

"Dad"—I cleared my throat—"if you're considering this. I want you to know that I think it's a great idea."

"I don't know if I can." He sighed and looked at my aunt.

"What's stopping you?" I asked though I had a feeling I knew the answer.

"What will happen to the house?" he asked. My father didn't like the idea of me having to care for him, but I feared the prospect of him not being able to take care of me in any capacity would be hard to accept.

"We could sell it," I said. It hurt to suggest it. I knew how proud Dad was of owning the house free and clear, but it was the only logical option.

"No." My father slammed the hand that wasn't holding Aunt Anita's hand on the table. "Your mother and I wanted you to have that house."

"Dad, that's really nice, but you know I couldn't afford to keep the house on my own."

"Nina and I could rent the house," Spencer chimed in. "We're renting now. You could use the income to pay your rent here and your property taxes."

Dad seemed to consider the idea.

I pulled out my phone and sent Spencer a text.

ME: AND WHERE WOULD I LIVE WHEN YOU AND NINA MOVE INTO MY HOUSE?

TEACHER'S PET: WE COULD RENT YOU A ROOM AT A COMPETITIVE RATE, AND IF YOU COULDN'T AFFORD IT, I COULD THINK OF OTHER FORMS OF COMPENSATION.

ME: EXCUSE ME, SIR?

TEACHER'S PET: (SMILING DEVIL HORN EMOJI)

"I'm sorry. I have to check on my students." I got up again and walked around the rec center, but I kept sneaking glances at the table. By the time I returned, Dad had agreed to move to Seven Palms and live with Aunt Anita. Though I was still processing this bombshell the two people who raised me dropped in my lap, I was really happy for Dad and felt like a huge weight had been lifted.

AT THE END OF THE MOST MENTALLY EXHAUSTING field trip I'd ever been a part of, I was standing outside the school bus talking to Sabrina.

"Did you know?" I asked her.

She made a circle around her face with her index finger.

"Does it look like I knew? Hell no, I didn't know. We could've been sisters this whole time."

"We were sisters this whole time," I reminded her.

"True. True." She hit me a sly grin. "So, things are going *well* with Mr. Jones."

"You make everything sound dirty, Brina."

"Excuse me, ma'am?" She pulled out her phone and showed me the text messages I sent her the night of the lockdown.

Rube: Spencer is safe. He and Nina are spending the night at my house.

Rube: btw, it *definitely* still works. (Winking face emoji)

We shared a laugh.

"Are you happy, Rube?"

"Yeah, I'm happy." I nodded.

"Good. Promise me you won't waste twenty years of your life like the horny old fools that raised us."

"Ugh, I still can't get over it." I shuddered. "Do you think they did it while we were in the house?"

"Girl, who knows?" She shook her head. "Anyway, go get on your bus. I'll make sure Pop gets home safe and sound."

"Love you, sis," I said in a singsong voice as I backed away from her.

"Haha. Shut up. I love you too."

DAD WAS HAVING DINNER AT THE SEVEN PALMS, SO I accepted Nina's invitation to eat with her and Spencer at their soon-to-be former home.

The grown-ups were in the kitchen cooking dinner while the kid was sprawled out on the living room floor watching Super Hero Girls.

"Thank you for the very nice thing you did for my dad today." I planted a kiss on his lips. "But we definitely should've had a conversation about moving in together first."

"You're absolutely right, beautiful. I got carried away, seeing Anita and Jack together. I knew he was so close to saying yes."

My heart melted at the thought of him being so invested in my father's happiness.

"But if it makes you comfortable, Nina and I will stay here."

"And pay my dad's rent?" I asked. Spencer shrugged and nodded. "That's ridiculous."

"If it would make you happy, it's not ridiculous." He kissed me again and went back to stirring the sauce on the stove. My chest tightened with emotion, and I drew in a deep breath to keep myself from crying into the garlic bread I was slicing.

What had I done right in my life to deserve the love of this man and his daughter?

I put my hand on the arm Spencer wasn't using to cook. His eyebrows shot up in question, and he looked at me.

"I love you," I said.

"I'm sorry. What was that, Miss Hayes." Spencer grinned down at me. "I'm not sure I heard you correctly."

"I love you."

"I love you, too." He said this as if it were the most obvious thing in the world. I knew that he must have loved me for a while and was waiting until I was ready to hear it. I felt like I was floating. He wrapped his arm around my waist, pulled me close, and kissed me. This kiss was more chaste than usual, with Nina in our sightline, but no less full of the passion it conveyed. When our lips finally separated, he asked, "Does this mean that you're ready to speed things up?"

"It does." I grinned.

"How fast are we talking?"

"I don't want to waste years of my life like my dad and Aunt Anita. I want everything. I want you, Nina, your family in Chicago, living in my house together... Everything."

"Are you sure?" He raised his eyebrow mischievously.

"Ummm, yes, Spencer. I'm sure." I narrowed my eyes at him. "What's going on?"

He released my waist, stepped back, and clapped his hands twice over his head.

"Little Bit," he called into the living room.

"Yeah, Daddy?"

"It's time to give Ruby your gift."

"It is?" she asked, and her dad nodded. "Finally! I'll go get it." She jumped to her feet and took off running to her room. I turned to watch her zoom past, and when I turned back to Spencer to ask him what the hell was going on, he was kneeling in front of me holding a ring.

It was a heart-shaped ruby flanked by two large diamonds set in platinum.

"Whoa." I looked at Spencer, and he had tears in his eyes, which immediately triggered my tears.

"Ruby Emma Hayes, will you make me the happiest, the most exhausted, and the most punctual man in the world and marry me?"

"How long have you been carrying that around?"

"Since Chicago."

"That was almost a month ago." I laughed, and tears sprung from my eyes. "Spencer, I really wanna say yes."

"Then, you should say yes." He grinned at me.

"I should tell you something first." My heart started pounding. I couldn't believe I was contemplating ruining this perfect moment, but things were moving so fast. Spencer and I couldn't take another step forward without him knowing everything.

"Okay." He nodded. "Can I get off of my knee first?"

"Yes." I laughed. Spencer stood, wrapped his arm around my waist, and slipped the ring on my finger. "Wait, you didn't hear what I had to tell you."

"Ruby, it won't matter, but if I change my mind, I'll take the ring back." He shrugged before grinning at me.

"So," I sighed. "I have a lot of student loan debt."

"Okay." He nodded. "Is that it?"

I wasn't expecting that response. I continued.

"No." I swallowed a lump in my throat. "When Dad had his stroke, there were a lot of things that his insurance wouldn't pay for, and I had just started teaching. I didn't have a lot of money. So, I maxed out my credit. I have a plan to pay it off, but I will probably die of old age before that happens." I bit my lip and looked up at him.

He crooked his finger under my chin and pulled it up so I could see him clearly. "So you thought I wouldn't want to marry you because you went into debt getting an education, and you maxed out your credit taking care of your father, who was sick?"

"Maybe?" I shrugged. "So, do you still want to marry me?'

"Baby, I want to marry you even more than I did before you told me."

"Well, that's good." I grinned and kissed him. "Because you were going to have to fight me to get this ring back."

Spencer burst out laughing just as Nina returned, holding a small velvet box.

"What's so funny?" she asked, glancing between her dad and me.

"Look." Spencer held up my hand.

"You said yes?" She looked at me. "You're gonna marry my daddy?"

"Yes." I nodded.

She crashed into me and wrapped her arms around my waist.

"Give Ruby your gift," Spencer said.

I gently removed her arms from my waist, crouched down to her eye level and saw that there were tears in her eyes.

"Oh, sweetie, don't cry."

"But I'm so happy." She sniffled. "I knew it. I knew it was you." Little tears spilled from her eyes, and I became a blubbering mess.

"Come here, Little Bit." Spencer scooped her in his arms and hugged her until she calmed down before setting her on the kitchen island, where she finally handed me the velvet box.

I opened it, and inside was a delicate gold chain threaded through what looked like a penne noodle but also made of gold.

"This is...this is..." My throat constricted, and I couldn't form words.

"Do you like it?" Nina asked.

"I love it," I whispered and handed the box to Spencer so he could put the necklace on me.

"My aunt made it. She said I gave her the idea." Nina beamed at me.

"Simi is rolling out an entire collection of jewelry inspired by Nina's necklaces next year for Mother's Day. This is the prototype, and it's one of a kind, just like you... There." He planted a kiss on my shoulder after he'd fastened the necklace.

"Okay, Little Bit. Dinner's almost ready. Go wash your hands." He helped her off of the counter, and she ran to the bathroom.

"How are you feeling?"

"Happy. Overwhelmed, but happy." I pressed our lips together. "I forgot to tell you one thing that might make you change your mind."

"Oh yeah?"

"I could never be a Bulls fan."

"Give me my ring back."

"No." I narrowed my eyes and took off, running around the island towards the living room. Spencer caught me around the waist and we collapsed onto the couch, where he kissed me and tickled me until I squealed for him to stop.

"Damn, I love you, Ruby."

"I love you too, Spencer."

THE END

TEN

SPENCER

EPILOGUE

"How are you always so horny?" I rolled onto my back panting and pulled my sweaty wife into the crook of my arm.

"I don't know. It's all these damn hormones. It's like my body doesn't understand that we can't get pregnant because we're already pregnant." She laughed. "And then it will say 'Hey, remember how sexy your husband looked holding that baby last weekend?' Then I have to attack you until my lust is sated, sir." She shot me a lascivious grin and kissed me. "How are you able to keep up with me?"

"That's why I don't miss a workout and keep myself hydrated. Your boy has to stay ready." I laughed. "Plus, you are a very sexy pregnant woman. It's not that difficult to want to sate your lust, my lady." I kissed her. "So, are you ready for today?"

"No." She glowered. "I mean, I'm happy. It still takes a little getting used to."

Ruby's dad and Sabrina's mom are getting married today. They've been living together at the Seven Palms for a year and a couple months ago decided they wanted to get married.

"We're gonna have to get ready to go soon." I was picking my sister up from the airport. She designed the jewelry for the ceremony and, for some reason, insisted on flying in to attend. She's gotten to know Ruby's family over the last year and loves any excuse to hang out with Nina.

I wrapped my arms around my wife and palmed her belly.

"Hey, did I ever tell you I made a playlist for you when I was in the lockdown?"

"No. Is that why your phone died?" She punched me in the chest.

"You're still mad about that?" I laughed because I knew that Ruby was joking, but she didn't realize that making that playlist for her kept me sane in that closet. Maybe that's why I kept it from her. I knew every moment I endured in that tiny dark box brought me closer to seeing her and Nina again.

The therapist I'd been seeing for the last year—paid for by my company in exchange for not suing them, along with a settlement we used to pay off Ruby's student loans—has helped me process the events of that day. I still get nervous in small spaces, and the only real argument I've had with my wife is when I tried—unsuccessfully—to persuade her to quit teaching and homeschool Nina when I found out we were expecting. After what I went through, it was hard for me to stomach the idea of them sitting in a school building all day, like fish in a barrel. I'm getting better, and I love that I can laugh with my wife about it. Laughter is truly the best medicine, especially when it comes from Ruby Jones.

"I will never stop being mad about that." She pouted until I kissed her. "What did you call it?"

"Love Jones." I laughed.

"Boo!" She laughed. "Seriously? You missed the opportunity to call your playlist Trapped in the Closet."

I burst out laughing, and she joined me.

"I'm so glad I married you," I said between chuckles.

"Me too." She sighed.

I laughed again, then stopped. "Hey, was that a Chicago crack?"

"No," she replied sarcastically before saying, "Yes."

"You know there's more to Chicago than Oprah Winfrey and R. Kelly, right?"

"Yeah, isn't Kanye from Chicago?" She tucked her teeth between her lips to keep from laughing.

"Give me my ring back," I joked and tickled her. We had a running joke that I would ask for my ring back whenever she talked slick about my hometown. It belonged in the hall of fame of empty threats. Every time I saw my wife, my eyes would dart to her hand, and the thrill of seeing my ring there never got old. I think she knew and that was why she teased me so often, and I'd never got tired of it.

"Of course, I know there's more to Chicago. It's my second favorite place in the world, and half of my family lives there." She smiled and turned her body to face mine. She wasn't joking about half of her family living in Chicago. I think she talked to my mother more than I did.

"Oh yeah? Where is your favorite place?"

"Right here." She ran her fingertips over the curve of my cheeks and brought our faces together. "With you."

"Hmm." I bopped her nose. "And you say I'm corny." I kissed her.

"Shut up." She laughed again. "So let me see this playlist… There better not be any R. Kelly on here."

I opened the Spotify app and handed her my phone.

"Let's see…" She brushed the pad of her fingertip over my screen. "Oh, *Kissing You* by TOTAL, a little on the nose, isn't it? *Lady* by D'Angelo, nice. *Angel* by Anita Baker, a classic. Oh, *Anniversary*. My parents used to dance to this song all the time. *Love of My Life*, really?" She cut her eyes at me.

"Yep." I pressed our lips together

"*Me and Mrs. Jones?*" She gave me a skeptical look. "You were making big plans in that closet, Mr. Jones."

"You know it, Mrs. Jones." I grabbed her left hand and brought her rings to my lips. I had Simi design her engagement ring to complement her mother's wedding ring. The same ring she tried to use to scare me away was the same ring I slipped on her finger at the same beach in California we're headed to today.

MY ENTIRE FAMILY FLEW OUT FROM CHICAGO TO watch us get married because Ruby was concerned about her dad making the trip east. They were happy to oblige, and Sarai's parents were even in attendance, which meant the world to us.

I was nervous about Sarai's parents meeting Ruby when they flew out to visit us a couple months before the wedding, but I didn't have to be. Ruby insisted they stay with us so they could spend as much time with Nina as possible. On the second morning of their visit, I came downstairs to find Ruby and Sarai's mother, Uba, talking in the kitchen over coffee. Before the end of their stay, Uba had taught Ruby how to make Kac Kac, a Somali dessert. Sarai got me addicted to them when we were dating, and Nina and I haven't had them since we left Chicago.

"WE HAVE TO GET UP SOON, BABE."

My wife hooked her leg around my waist and brought us as close together as she could with her belly in the way.

"Maybe one more time?" She tucked her bottom lip between her teeth.

"You're trying to kill me, aren't you?" I narrowed my eyes at her.

"You've escaped death before. I like your odds." She giggled and kissed me before taking my hand and closing it over one of her breasts. They'd grown significantly over the last few months, but they were still soft, smooth, and the perfect size for the palm of my hand.

I grabbed my phone with my free hand and tapped one of the songs in my playlist. *Ask of You* started to play through our Bluetooth speakers, and I began to sing to my wife.

"Kissing you…"

"You are so silly!" She laughed.

"…I'm a big boy…"

"Yes, you are," she said in a deep sultry voice.

She burst into her melodic laugh, and I spent the rest of the song kissing her everywhere, and yes, even there.

THE WEDDING WAS SHORT AND BLISSFUL. WE WERE blessed with beautiful weather, and I spent the reception watching my six-year-old daughter drop it like it was room temperature on the dance floor and holding my wife on my lap with one palm on her belly.

"Brina and Simi really hit it off, huh?" I asked Ruby.

"Babe, seriously?" She giggled.

"What?"

"I can neither confirm nor deny anything, but I know Brina has produced three high profile events in Chicago in the last two months and is considering a very lucrative offer from a Chicago-based firm."

"Well." I nodded. "It will be good that Brina already has a friend there." I tightened my arms around her belly.

"Oh, you sweet summer child." She kissed my temple. "Do you need me to send you a text message?" She giggled.

"What?" Then the realization dawned. "Oh. Oh! Nice! How long has this been going on?"

"I'm not sure, but at least since our wedding."

"Why haven't they said anything?"

She shrugged. "I don't know about Simi, but Brina has always been like that. In high school, I didn't know she had a boyfriend until she brought him to prom, and they had been together for six months."

"I know Simi has been a little wary of relationships since her divorce." I nodded.

Ruby and I lifted our water glasses and toasted to Jack and Anita, to Sabrina and Simi, and to ourselves.

"Whew!" Nina flopped into a chair next to mine. "My dogs are bar-king!" My wife and I had a good idea where Nina was learned this new phrase.

Ruby and I shot a look at Sabrina, who shrugged at us, and the four of us burst out laughing.

"Thank you, baby," Ruby moaned, and I swung her swollen feet into my lap on our couch and began to massage them. "My dogs were bar-king!"

We burst out laughing.

"What are we gonna do with that little girl?"

"I don't even know," she said in a sigh when her laughter died down.

"She should start getting ready for bed soon."

"Five more minutes, please," she begged, and finding it completely impossible to deny this woman anything, I continued to rub.

Ten minutes later, we tapped on Nina's door, which was Ruby's old bedroom.

"Time to get ready for bed, Little Bit," I said.

"Okay, can I finish watching Mommy's video?"

"Of course," Ruby answered with a smile, and I saw her fingers drift to her necklace. Simi had Nina's original creations framed for a wedding present along with the photo of Ruby and me wearing them. Every time I looked at that photo, I couldn't believe that I didn't realize that I was falling in love with her, even then.

She hasn't watched all of Sarai's videos, but she's seen a couple. Again, I was nervous at first, but Ruby never ceases to amaze me. Ruby and Sarai were completely different people, but a small part of me felt that if they'd met when Sarai was still with us, they'd be really good friends.

"—why you have to wash your makeup brushes often," Sarai's voice called from Nina's tablet. "This is highlighter. Very important. Now, you only use highlighter to accentuate or enhance your nose, never to minimize it. Your daddy and I worked very hard to give you that nose."

I felt Ruby chuckle in my arms.

"Don't ever let anyone tell you it's not beautiful…"

When the video ended, Nina put her tablet down, rubbed Ruby's belly for luck, and made her way to the bathroom. I pulled Ruby into Nina's room, lowered myself onto the bed, pulled her into my lap, and picked up the tablet.

"I wanna show you something." I looked into her eyes, trying to gauge her reaction. My heart started racing, and she put her soft hand on my cheek to calm me.

"Okay." She smiled. I scrolled through the videos until I found the one I was looking for and hit play.

I had only seen this video once. Two years ago, I edited and uploaded it for Sarai. She was still alive then: living, breathing, bossing me around and making me laugh until my cheeks hurt. I was still in denial and still hoping for some miracle cure or treatment that would end our daily nightmare, so we could erase all these videos and pretend her cancer never happened.

Tonight seemed like the perfect time to watch it again, and I had the perfect person to watch it with me. This was one of the last videos Sarai made. She was sitting in a hospital bed, very thin and frail, but she was in full makeup, wearing a bright purple head wrap, the green elephant pendant Nina picked out for her, and the giant gold hoops Simi made with at least a dozen bangles on each arm. I drew in a deep breath and let it out slowly. This was the version of Sarai I tried to push away. She was weak and in so much pain but still trying to put on a brave front. Trying to make sure everyone else was okay.

"Hey, Teeny Tiny! It's your mommy here. I'm going to make a very important video today. I know Daddy and Ayeeyo have told you that I'm going to Heaven soon."

My eyes started to sting, and I felt Ruby smoothing her palm over my back.

"And I don't want you to worry, because it's going to be sunny and beautiful and my ayeeyo will be there, and I will be able to eat all the Kac Kac I want, whenever I want, without getting a tummy ache. Doesn't that sound great?" Sarai flashed one of her dazzling grins at the camera.

I wiped away a tear and looked up to see that Ruby was tearing up too. She gave me a small smile.

"But when I'm done eating all of the Kac Kac in Heaven, I'm going to do something very important, and I need your help, okay. I'm going to start looking for an angel to take care of you and Daddy for me."

I heard Ruby sniffle and tears were streaming down her face.

"You okay, baby? Do you want me to stop?" I reached out and brushed away a tear with the backs of my fingertips.

"No, I'm fine." She sniffled and kissed my temple.

"I'll need your help because after I'm gone, Daddy is going to miss me a lot and be really sad, so he may not see the angel. So, I'm depending on you to keep your eyes peeled for her, okay? How will you know she's the angel? I'm glad you asked."

Sarai grinned again.

"I made a list."

She held up a small pad.

"The angel will be very pretty. She will smile whenever she looks at you. Daddy will smile whenever he looks at her. You will always know that she loves you when you look in her eyes, even if you're being naughty. She will be so funny. One of her favorite things to do will be to make you and Daddy laugh. The angel will also be very smart, so she'll have lots of things to teach you.

"So, if you meet someone that is all of those things, then you must be very nice to her because she might be the angel that Mommy sent for you."

She laid the pad in her lap, took a deep breath, and looked off-camera. Uba appeared in the frame and held up a water glass with a plastic straw for Sarai to sip.

"Now, if you are the angel and you happen to be watching this video, I want to thank you for taking care of my family. I'll never meet you, but I know you must be an extraordinary person…and very patient." She laughed, and Ruby gave a watery chuckle and nodded. I tightened my arm around her waist.

"Please make sure Nina doesn't wrap her father around her little finger…"

"Too late." Ruby chuckled again.

"And please make sure Spencer gets enough sleep, gets to his appointments on time, and remembers to stop and enjoy the little things in life…"

"Done," Ruby said.

"Except the sleep."

"Hush."

"And if it's not too much to ask." Sarai paused. "Please don't let her forget me."

Two glistening tears streaked down her face, and she quickly wiped them away before taking a deep breath and smiling at the camera.

"And if you hurt my family, I will figure out a way to come back and haunt you."

Ruby burst out laughing.

"I don't know how yet, but one day you'll try some foolishness, and the lights will flicker, and that will be me." Sarai glared at the camera before bursting into giggles. Ruby was still laughing.

"Oh, Sarai, that's too much," Uba's voice called from off-camera.

"What, Mom? I'm joking…or am I?" She waggled her eyebrows at the camera before bursting into a coughing fit. Uba rushed to give her more water. Sarai cleared her throat and continued. "The woman that falls in love with my goofy-butted husband will have to have a sense of humor, or she's not gonna last."

"Where is the lie?" Ruby murmured.

"Please." I sucked my teeth. "I'm not goofy."

"You are the goofiest." She sniffled and kissed the side of my head.

"Mom, can you turn off the camera?" Sarai pointed at the lens.

"It's off," Uba said.

"No, it isn't. The red light is on. That means it's recording."

"No, green means go. Red means stop."

"Well, this camera didn't get that memo, so please..." She gestured to the lens again.

Ruby giggled, and I smiled.

"Ugh, with this foolishness." Uba approached the camera and was blocking the lens with her body.

"Now, which button is it?"

"The big one."

"This one?"

"No, the big one."

"Sarai, there's only one big button. Is it—"

The video ended.

Ruby was still laughing and wiping away tears.

I remember wanting to edit that part of the video out, but Sarai wouldn't let me. I didn't understand until after she was gone.

It wasn't the carefully staged and prepped photos and videos you treasure the most when you lose someone special. It's the random and candid moments that showed you who the people you loved really were. That's the way you remember them.

Ruby once told me her fondest memories of her mother were of her reheating the same cup of tea in the microwave for three hours every morning but never finishing it. She also missed the way her mom would always close the oven door with her foot and how it would drive Jack crazy whenever she did it.

I took a deep breath and tossed the tablet on the bed, wrapped both arms around my wife, and pressed our lips together. Her kiss tasted salty, sweet, and like a lifetime of answered prayers.

"Thank you for sharing that with me." She smiled and pressed our foreheads together.

"Thank you for being our angel."

Nina Jones age 5 + a haf

THE SOUNDTRACK

AN ANGEL FOR DADDY

The An Angel for Daddy playlist on Spotify can be found at bit.ly/AngelforDaddy.

1. KISSIN' YOU - TOTAL
2. UNTITLED (HOW DOES IF FEEL) - D'ANGELO
3. ANGEL - ANITA BAKER
4. LADY - D'ANGELO
5. ANNIVERSARY - TONY! TONI! TONÉ!
6. LOVE OF MY LIFE (AN ODE TO HIP HOP) - ERYKAH BADU, COMMON
7. ME AND MRS. JONES - BILLY PAUL
8. JONZ IN MY BONZ - D'ANGELO
9. TELL ME - GROVE THEORY
10. ANGEL OF MINE - MONICA

11. SOON AS I GET HOME - BABYFACE
12. TEACHME - MUSIQ SOULCHILD
13. LOVE JONES - BRIGHTER SIDE OF DARKNESS
14. KISS OF LIFE - SADE

AUTHOR'S NOTE

Dearest Reader,

Thank you for reading An Angel for Daddy.

This book was originally inspired by old episode of The Oprah Winfrey Show about a mother who upon discovering she was dying of cancer made a series of videos for her daughter and husband.

This story is also inspired by the countless brave souls who find love after loss.

If you love stories about adorable kids, hot single parents, meddling but loving family members & two lost souls finding love after loss then you will love Everything's Better with Lisa! And lucky you, there's an excerpt on the next page!

Thank you:

My amazing critique partner, Marina Garcia. I wrote this book in five days due, largely, in part to our nightly writing sprint marathons.

My amazing beta readers who gave me amazing feed back and the confidence in my tiny little story. Again, please stop messaging me to tell me my romantic comedy novelette made you cry.

Tasha L. Harrison for creating the #20kin5Days challenge that made this story possible. Thank you for continually convincing me that I can do things that I don't think I'm capable of. Your ingenuity and encouragement continues to inspire me and I am so lucky to know you.

Stacey Agdern for helping me to create this adorable blurb that I'm in love with at the very last minute. Thank you for being a great friend and cheerleader. I can't wait to create amazing things with you so I can read them.

Rhonda Merwath for squeezing my teeny tiny book into your crazy schedule at the last minute. When I thought my story was perfect you pushed me to make it better & it worked. Thank you for being the other half of my brain, sexy Darth Vader.

Hellhoney for bringing Nina, Spencer and Ruby to life with this gorgeous illustration.

My genius and brutally honest mother. Thank you for being my Stroke & Vascular Dementia technical advisor.

My ARC team for giving their time and energy to read my work and help spread the word.

Thank you so much, dear reader, for reading An Angel for Daddy!

I hope you liked it. Please consider leaving a review on Goodreads or wherever you share your good news!

September 2019 & September 2021

xoxo,

lucy

ERYTHING'S

better

WITH LISA

UNNY DRAMATIC STEAMY
NOVEL BY

UCY EDEN

—

ONE: COLE

—

2-6-5-3. Red X.

"Fuck!"

2-6-5-3. Red X.

"Shit!"

I typed my code into the keypad a third time with no success.

"Goddammit!" I kicked the wood doorframe of the hundred-year-old Harlem brownstone I'd called home for the past six years.

"Hey, asshole! Shut the fuck up!" a female voice shouted from the ground-level apartment.

I looked over the banister to see a short woman with waist-length, chestnut-colored hair staring up at me, holding a baseball bat.

"Crystal?" It was too dark to see her clearly. I was definitely more than a little buzzed, and my biological mother was the only short woman with long dark brown hair I knew. But why was she holding a baseball bat, and why was her voice different?

With a little difficulty, I walked down the stairs to get a closer look. The woman took a step back as I approached and held the bat higher, tightening her grip on the neck.

"My name is not Crystal, and I live here."

Upon closer inspection—as close as I could get without getting clocked in the head, anyway—I could tell she definitely wasn't Crystal. She was younger, way more beautiful, and she didn't have my birth mother's bright blue eyes. Crystal also moved back to Missouri four years ago. Most importantly, tiny Babe Ruth definitely didn't live in my house. I was drunk, but not that drunk.

"You live in here?" That wasn't exactly how I meant to phrase that, but my brain and my mouth weren't cooperating. Also, I'd become aware that I was leaning against the brick wall of the stoop to support my weight.

"Yes," gorgeous, not-Crystal hissed. "I live here." She was so sincere that I was hit with a wave of confusion, and when it ebbed, realization slapped me in the face. I took a step back and looked up at the door I had been kicking a moment ago, then I looked to the right at the door I should've been kicking.

"Shit." I did it again. I went to the wrong fucking house.

Why did these brownstones all look the same?

I turned to head to the brownstone where my code would work, and I guess I turned too fast because I stumbled and had to grab the railing to keep from crashing to the ground.

"Are you okay?" She lowered her bat, but she didn't take a step forward. I was drunk. I was trying to enter the wrong house, and I had almost busted my ass in front of my sexy neighbor.

"I'm fine, *Crystal.* Mind your business." This ordeal was embarrassing enough without Batgirl, suddenly concerned for my welfare.

Hadn't she just called me an asshole?

I didn't need her help. I was a grown-ass man who needed to walk twenty feet to his front door.

"Excuse me?" she said. "Again, dickhead, my name is not Crystal, and you screaming in the middle of the night woke me up from my much-needed sleep, so it is my business."

I turned to face her and felt myself sway as I tried to stabilize. Her outburst was sexy as fuck and I felt an overwhelming urge to kiss her.

Nope. Nope.

That was definitely the alcohol talking.

I can't kiss her.

I have to get home.

The word *home* floated to my consciousness, but instead of focusing on that goal, I decided to speak.

"You kind of look like my mother, but not really. Her name is Crystal. I'm fine. Just got confused. My house looks exactly like my sister's house." I pointed at the brownstone next door before pointing at Kimmy's.

"Your sister?" She gave me the look, the skeptical look I get when I tell people about my family. One would think I'd gotten used to it after all these years. Maybe it was all the tequila shots, but tonight it pissed me off. She continued, "The woman that owns this brownstone is not your sister, and I'm not your mother, so you need to take your drunk ass home, to your actual house, before I call the cops."

"Kimbery Shimmins is my shishter!" I yelled as I backed away from her towards my house. I could hear myself slurring my words and considered the possibility that trying to walk and talk at the same time wasn't the best idea. I turned toward my house, continuing to amble forward. "And I'm glad you're not my mom because my mom is awesome, and you'd be a shitty mom with your baseball bat and your potty mouth."

Even though I was sure I just used the words "potty mouth," I knew I'd said something profound because I was met with silence.

I turned to look at her and found her expression blank. A loud and expletive-filled response was what I expected, but she just stood there, frozen and a little sad. A feeling like regret crept over me, but I couldn't figure out what I should have felt regretful about. I tried to replay the last thing I said, but I couldn't fucking remember, something about Kimberly and a shitty potty?

That look... I couldn't stand seeing it, so I turned away from her and climbed the steps to my door, where I typed in the four-digit code.

Green checkmark.

— — —

Thank you for reading this bonus chapter of Everything's Better with Lisa. Visit geni.us/EBWL

ALSO BY LUCY EDEN

DON'T MISS MY NEXT RELEASE!

Sign up for my newsletter for updates & freebies.

CLICK HERE TO SIGN UP OR VISIT LUCYEDEN.COM

ABOUT THE AUTHOR

Lucy Eden is the *nom de plume* of a romance obsessed author who writes the kind of romance she loves to read. She's a sucker for alphas with a soft gooey center, over the top romantic gestures, strong & smart MCs, humor, love at first sight (or pretty damn close), happily ever afters & of course, steamy love scenes.

When Lucy isn't writing, she's busy reading—or listening to—every book she can get her hands on—romance or otherwise.

She lives in New York with her husband, two children, a turtle & a Yorkshire Terrier.

CPSIA information can be obtained
at www.ICGtesting.com
Printed in the USA
BVHW071445291121
622764BV00011B/806